MOG

BRONZE AGE NEANDERTHAL

AN EPIC NOVEL
BOOK TWO OF THE
BRONZE AGE WARRIOR SERIES

AN ORIGINAL STORY BY
BUD SELIGSON

Lost Age Publishing
2017

Printed in the United States of America

Cover Art and Interior design by: Cyrusfiction Productions.

ISBN: 978-1-946480-10-1

9018 Balboa Boulevard
Suite #562
Northridge, CA 91325

WARNING

This novel is a "really hot book"—and it contains sexually explicit scenes. This is also a combination work of fact and fiction, woven together as a product of the author's imagination.

"What we have here is a riddle wrapped in a mystery inside of an enigma."

—Winston Churchill

Dedicated to my wife, Diane. If I listed all the many ways that she has helped me, this dedication would be larger than the novel.

All my love,
Bud

SOME INTERESTING THOUGHTS
FROM THE AUTHOR

The biggest question about history is "why did it happen this way"?

Is it all a chaotic system in which things happen in a random way?

The idea that the world is illusory goes back many thousands of years.

The linearity of human existence makes aging and death irreversible.

Truth changes with the special perspective of the beholder.

Science is nothing but trained and well-organized common sense.

A leader must be a fox to recognize traps and a lion to frighten off the wolves.

The day-to-day condition of mankind … is a condition of war of everyone against everyone.

It is people who give "style" to the times and events going on around them.

Conclusion from history: war alone raises all of human energy to the highest pitch and stamps with nobility the people who have the courage to make it.

When a man sits with a pretty girl for an hour, it seems like a minute—but let him sit on a hot stove for a minute and that minute is longer than any hour. This is relativity.
—Albert Einstein

After concluding this trilogy—one of the most compelling examples of human history anywhere— your mind will keep spinning with the question, "Did this really happen, and if so, what…?"

Science fiction/fantasy is a literature of infinite possibilities.…

And finally, I leave you with a quote from Benjamin Franklin:

"For the want of a nail the shoe was lost, For the want of a shoe the horse was lost, For the want of a horse the rider was lost, For the want of a rider the battle was lost, For the want of a battle the kingdom was lost, And all for the want of a horseshoe-nail."

I would like to try and open the door to a time long ago and attempt to reveal an age of wonder and danger at the dawn of our ancestors who were the first modern humans.

We should all be aware that the label that we have given ourselves, *Homo sapiens*, means "man the wise." We all must sometimes wonder about the accuracy of this label.

—Bud Seligson

BRONZE AGE NEANDERTHAL

BY
BUD SELIGSON

PROLOGUE

This is a dark age, a very bloody age: an age of violence and great lovemaking.

It is a land of giant mountains, mighty rivers, icy landscapes, and dark forests.

From their enigmatic beginnings, through their first tests as warriors and leaders, both Atia and Mog hold the destiny of the world some 5,300 years ago in their capable hands.

I am bringing back, from the first of the two novels in the *Bronze Age Warrior Series*, previously written pages in order to allow us to recall exactly where we left off.

It is important to our story to remember just what it was that was so world-shaking and so important in our cultural shaping that came down to us from these early days when our *Homo sapiens* story was just getting started!

Of course, the following Chapter Forty-Eight from the first book in the series is all about our very special human females.

CHAPTER FORTY-EIGHT
from *ATIA: Bronze Age Warrior*

The human leaders were all gathered at the top of the highest of the small hills behind the well-armed soldiers. Everything they could think of that needed doing was already done. Now it was time to just wait and see what the day held in store for all of them.

There were plans in place for following a defeated

Neanderthal army back to their home base, and plans to hold back the winning Neanderthals if they came out of all of this as the winners. There was no doubt in any of the human leaders' minds that, unless Mog had come up with something that no one else had thought of, a victory was just waiting for the humans to claim.

The two armies were already on the field and moving about to get themselves ready. The humans were mostly sitting on the ground where they would be ready to fight at a moment's notice.

The Neanderthals had two unusual things going on in the area where they were gathered, which both surprised and worried the human leaders.

The first thing that they all noticed was a large raised platform standing about fifteen feet high. It was assumed that this was a viewing area for Mog and his officers from which to watch the battle. They would probably be sending orders out by messengers from this central control area to the formations.

The human command post was set up pretty much the same way except that they had gone one step further in their organization. They had divided their human warriors into six different sections with each section having a different color sash worn by the soldiers and their officers.

If, for example, the human commanders had an order for the red group, a messenger from the command post would rush over to the red group and give the order to the officer in charge of that particular location. Each of the human fighting groups had their own colors, which were black, blue, green, yellow and orange.

The Neanderthals were doing something different, also, which was that a large blocking sheet of material was in front of each Neanderthal as he marched out onto the battlefield and took up his position. The materials that were covering the front of each Neanderthal group were gray in color and were about seven feet high. They were like huge banners being held up in front of each group of fighters. If they had wanted to block off the humans from seeing their men lining up, they were very successful. This lack of clearly viewing the enemy had the human leadership quite nervous. What could they possibly be hiding behind those gray banners? Was this somehow Mog's response to the slingshot and the ballista?

Everyone was extremely nervous as the time slowly passed on its way to high noon, which was the scheduled starting time for the war to begin. High noon was picked because there could be no mistake as to the time when the sun in the sky was at its peak for the day.

There was not much longer to wait as an ominous quiet descended across both sides of the battlefield.

One of the many things that bothered Atia was the fact that he was far behind the fighting lines and would not be able to see exactly what would be happening when the two armies clashed on the field.

He had also kept Avoti out of the fight, as he was considered future leadership. Leadership did not fight as common foot soldiers.

The soldiers were armed with knives, swords, bows and arrows, slingshots, and some handheld spears that appeared here and there in the ranks.

Within minutes of the actual time of high noon, horns were sounded, and the human soldiers all got to their feet. The moment that they had all been waiting for had finally arrived. The soldiers all seemed rested and ready to fight as they tightened up their formations.

The battle plan was for them to advance only a little bit from their present positions. They were to go toward the middle of the field only far enough so that their lines were spread out evenly across the width of the area. They all knew to be very careful of the many potholes that were underfoot.

When the enemy was within firing range of the slingshot each soldier was now holding in a ready-to-fire position, the ballistas would fire and the field would be filled with flying material directed at the Neanderthals.

Besides the slingshots that each human held ready, a small shield was covering him in case of incoming arrow fire being directed at him. They had stolen this new idea from Mog. A great shout came bursting across the field as the Neanderthals received their marching orders.

The two sides very slowly picked their way across the pocketed ground.

The humans held their slingshots and shields in a ready position as they stood quietly and watched the slow advance of the Neanderthals. The Neanderthals slowly marched closer, with their blocking banners still held high and in place so that the humans could not clearly see the slowly advancing fighters. Everyone was wondering why this strange thing was being done, and they were only moments away from finding out the horrible truth that was waiting for them. The covering banners were finally dropped and trampled underfoot by the slowly advancing enemy.

The front-line human soldiers, as an entire group, suddenly held back firing their ready-to-shoot weapons. Coming at them were two thousand Neanderthal soldiers, which were expected and very well prepared for. The human soldiers were waiting for them. The long-awaited fight that they had trained so hard and long for was now upon them, and they were ready, very ready.

They all stared in horror, however. They could not believe what they were seeing. They now all knew what the clever thinking supreme leader Mog had come up with to counter the human advantage of the slingshot and the ballista.

What the human soldiers saw at the same moment, causing them all to back off from firing their weapons, was that each slowly advancing Neanderthal soldier had tied to the front of him a helpless, naked human female slave.

Each female was closely tied up, with her hands tied to the hands of each Neanderthal. They were physically attached and facing forward. Their feet were also tied ankle-to-ankle with the Neanderthals, so that each step and each move made by the Neanderthal soldier was matched exactly by the closely bound female.

The women were the blocking shields for the wickedly screaming Neanderthal soldiers as they marched forward in perfect lockstep toward the lines of the humans. Their evil smiles were just beaming from their ugly faces. They knew who had the advantage on the battlefield now, and they were enjoying themselves to the fullest. Each female hostage had a thick gag tied tightly in her mouth to stop her from screaming and warning the waiting human troops.

Mog had come up with the plan of gathering each and every female human slave from all over the Neanderthal world so that he had plenty of female humans to satisfy his needs. He spent weeks training his soldiers to learn how to move about with females tied up in front of them.

He had ordered each female stripped of all clothing.

Being naked was his way of showing the humans that all of the females attached to his men were human. He thought that he knew humans well enough to count on them not firing their weapons against other humans, especially females. It turned out that he was right, and that decision on his part turned the tide of the battle that day.

Mog had gone even one step further. He had given permission for each soldier to rape the captive female human assigned to him as often as he wished. The females and the soldiers, however, had to be kept apart for a minimum of four days before the battle day so that they all could be back at full strength. His troops loved Mog for giving them the use of the women, and his loyalty from his soldiers was one hundred percent. Mog had given no consideration to raped and highly abused female humans because to him they were just battle protection for his all-important fighters.

As it turned out, the result of having the human females in front of his Neanderthals, facing the human troops, turned out exactly as Mog had predicted.

The humans did not fire their ballistas or their slingshots. Not one shot was fired anywhere. Almost all of the human soldiers turned around and ran back toward the human settlements. They had no instructions as to what they were supposed to do in this situation, and so they just turned around and ran away.

The slowly advancing Neanderthals began firing hundreds of arrows into the backs of the fleeing humans, killing and wounding scores of them. It was all over within thirty minutes from start to finish, when a loud Neanderthal signal horn recalled the fighters back to camp. As ordered, they turned and started back toward their camp, singing victory songs as they moved along.

Mog had given standing orders for the soldiers to kill their still-attached human females, but most of the happy Neanderthal soldiers did not do so. It was true that the soldiers were beasts at heart, but as bad as they were, they were not bad enough to slaughter helpless females who had caused them no harm. These now-unattached females, most of whom were physically able to move and to help other former captives, followed the fleeing human fighters toward the safety of the human settlement.

By allowing these females to escape, Mog made his first really big mistake. This was a major blunder that would come back to haunt him. His foolishness in not having soldiers standing by to kill all human females right away, and allowing the females to flee the killing fields, cost Mog and his Neanderthals dearly.

Before this terrible day in their lives, most human females had never even dreamed of fighting for their own lives and the lives of their loved ones. Up to this moment they had never considered standing shoulder to shoulder with their male human partners. This had now changed forever.

We all know that there is nothing as fierce as a female lion when she is defending her mate or her cubs. The very same truth applies to our own human females. When Mog badly used, abused and destroyed so many of them on that terrible day of the battle, he caused them to demand and to get what they demanded. They demanded—and got—the complete extermination of the Neanderthal race at a later date in time.

Mog's Neanderthals soon found out what it was like to have a female human's deeply rooted hatred, which they inspired in our women on that fateful day. These human women, who were constantly raped and beaten by the Neanderthals, were determined to see the extermination of their hated enemy.

It was the women who absolutely refused to compromise with them to divide up the world between human and Neanderthal as Mog was going to suggest again and again. It was the women who demanded from their mates, lovers, sons and warriors that they continue the fight until every last one of the enemy was destroyed with no chance of their ever making a comeback.

As we all know, women never forget a terrible wrong done to them and never give up in their relentless pursuit of what is right and proper. This admirable human female trait has not changed over the generations, and we love them for it.

Play nice, play fair and play for real. This is the belief of the modern woman of today who was taught all of these things by their mothers and their mothers' mothers, going way back in the history of our race. This has allowed women to take their rightful place as full partners with their male counterparts in the world of today.

And very soon, if not quite yet, it will be women who make this world of ours a better place for all of us.

CHAPTER ONE

Mog was excited beyond belief. Never in his entire life had any of his many plans and schemes worked out as perfectly as he had just watched them do on the open battlefield.

Only minutes ago, on the huge flat area where his Neanderthal army had faced off against the overwhelmingly better-armed and better-trained forces of the humans, his forces had won the complete battle with absolutely no loss of Neanderthal lives!!!

It was very true that the way he had defeated the humans was underhanded and quite despicable, but after all, Mog and his soldiers were Neanderthals and they did not hold themselves up to the higher moral ground that the humans were always talking about.

Mog had his army generals recall their soldiers after they had finished cutting down hundreds of fleeing male and female humans, who had simply turned around and run away as fast as they could.

Mog left the final closure of the battle to his appointed staff and returned to his field office for a few minutes of quiet and a silent celebration.

It was during quiet moments like this that he missed his old female companion Kat, who would have known just what to do with Mog in order to calm him down from his recently highly charged emotions and wild thoughts that were running through his mind.

He knew that he needed to take himself away from the army camp that he had set up and search out a few friendly females, either human or Neanderthal, who would be able to take his racing mind off the day's earlier happenings.

He would have time to think about everything that had just happened at a later time. Right now, he knew that he needed to get laid and he knew just what part of the small town that surrounded his campsite he would head for.

❦ ❦ ❦

He had hired her for a full night's service. She looked extremely attractive to Mog when her handler introduced her to him.

She was an interesting mix of human and Neanderthal; the slave trader told him that the mother was kept around for breeding purposes.

He said that this one was the best to come along in a long time. Mixed-breeds were in high demand, and he agreed that Mog had made an excellent selection.

He also said that the girl was Mog's for the night as a complete courtesy from himself to Mog, the great leader. He did go on to say that Mog should not expect too much from her in that she was very young and was still learning her trade.

Mog upon hearing this was very pleased and told

the trader that he would be rewarded at a later time if the girl came up to his expectations.

಼ ಼ ಼

Her name was Candy, and she looked as sweet to Mog as her name implied. She was slender like a human female with big bulging breasts that pressed against the top she was wearing. Mog thought that she seemed to have the best parts from each of her parents who were human and Neanderthal.

Candy started to unbutton her top but Mog stopped her. The fun of being with a female was greatly increased for him when he did the undressing himself. Holding her gently so as not to hurt her, he guided them into the huge bed that was in the very center of the large room.

His lips quickly found hers. He seemed to be in a hurry to take this delightful young girl, and without any preliminary foreplay on his part, he probed her mouth with deep, unrelenting sweeps of his tongue.

She pressed her well-formed breasts up against him and surrendered herself to the wild passion of his kisses. Her only goal was to satisfy this huge customer and possibly get a generous tip from him when her services were finally concluded.

He leaned back and pulled her up until they both stood up on their knees in the center of the bed. After fumbling with the row of buttons at her back, he peeled the bodice from her trim torso, and she helped by wriggling her arms free of the sleeves. He found the laces of her stays, and impatiently yanked them loose, casting the entire undergarment aside within seconds and took her well-formed breasts in his hands through her thin summer coverall. He swallowed hard as he admired them, lifting and kneading the soft globes with his large fingers. He seemed to be lost in those curves—his touch unhurried, his breathing slow and thick.

Her nipples grew painfully hard, gathering into tight, prominent peaks that chafed against the fabric top that she was wearing. He eased her neckline down but the gap was not generous enough to afford him access to where he wanted to go. Instead, he bent his head and suckled her breasts straight through the covering.

Half-human, half-Neanderthal, his companion for the moment, Candy by name, was receiving the sensations of his soft tongue licking her breasts through the rough fabric, and it was suddenly so intensely pleasurable to her, that she could not help but moan out loud.

She reached for the hem of his shirt, tugging it free of his waistband and sliding her hands beneath the material, she felt the tight muscles of his abdomen and the faint trail of hair leading down to his groin.

Emboldened by his gruff sounds of approval, she slid her hand downward, grasping the rigid length of him that was tenting out from his pants. "You'll have to tell me what you like and what you want me to do," Candy said softly.

He raised his head from her breast, seemingly abandoning his efforts to undress her as he finished pulling his own shirt loose. "There aren't any rules here. If I do something to you and you enjoy it, then there will be a good chance that I'll enjoy it if you do the same thing to me." He finished taking off his shirt and threw it aside.

"Oh," she replied. "I understand!"

As he reached for the button holding his pants up, she bent forward and took one of his nipples into her own mouth, in the same aggressive manner that Mog had done to hers.

He hissed out his breath, and she instantly jerked back and away.

"Not good?" she asked.

"Good!" he assured her, as he slid one of his hands over her soft neck. "VERY, VERY GOOD! You are a fast learner!"

Smiling to herself, she bent and tried again, only this time she licked first, teasing HIS small, flat circle to a tiny bud.

He groaned as she fitted her lips around it, suckling gently, then nipping with her teeth.

"WOW!" he exclaimed in a loud voice.

A sudden heat surged between Candy's thighs. She had never felt so sensual, and so powerful as she now did with this powerful male Neanderthal.

"Enough of that," he said as he took her hand and pressed it firmly down to his groin.

"Lie down," he said and down she went.

With focused concentration, he divested her of stockings, petticoat and almost all of her undergarments until she lay atop the sheets clad only in a very thin see-through slip. The dampened slip clung to her nipples as feverish breaths lifted her chest in an up and down motion as she kept gasping for breath.

He sat on the edge of the bed and wrestled briefly with his boots and the rest of his clothing until he was completely naked. Fully undressed now, he straddled her thighs with his proud, thick shaft jutting out from a nest of black hair. "I must have you," he muttered, forcing her thighs wide and thrusting into her quivering core.

She gasped at the fresh spear of pain mingling with the ebbing wave of pleasure.

With short digs of his hips, he pushed further and further into her.

Her tender flesh ached and stretched. Just when she thought she couldn't possibly take any more of-him, he grasped her backside in both of his gigantic hands, angled her hips differently, and sank deeper still. Her neck arched as she struggled for breath. She was so full of him that she felt him to be everywhere inside of her. At last he was fully located as he rested atop her for a moment, panting against the curve of her neck.

The joining hurt her, but it also felt indescribably right. She knew that she was a woman and that she was made for this kind of loving. She was loving the fact that she could take him inside her and hold him there so tightly that there was nowhere else that the great Mog would rather be right at that moment than here on top of her willing body.

Kissing her softly, he began to thrust again, gently now. Her body adjusted to his and he began to move easily, gliding in and out with smooth, powerful strokes.

Within seconds, the act ceased hurting so much and began to feel warm, and quite pleasant indeed. She relaxed her thighs, spreading her legs a bit wider yet to take him in deeper. She was reveling in the weight of his body atop hers and the firmness of his muscled shoulders and the moist sleekness of his back.

As the tempo increased, she ran her hands possessively over the hard angles and planes of his back, and even daring to cup the taut, flexing muscles of his buttocks. He suddenly made a gruff sound, and she sensed a shift in him. Consideration was banished from him, and raw need took its place.

He rose up on his knees, lifting her hips from the bed in his strong, sculpted hands. The tendons in his neck stood out like ropes. Her breasts jounced wildly as he pistoned his hips, taking her hard and fast in ruthless pursuit of his own pleasure. He made a rough noise, something between a growl and a moan.

And then he collapsed atop her, shuddering and helpless in the throes of his release.

She wrapped her arms around his shoulder, smoothing the damp hair from his brow.

He made a brief pillow of her breasts and spoke her name again in a soft voice as if he was memorizing it for future use. It was only minutes until he was up, dressed and gone out the door. The only sign that he had been there was the huge amount of gold coins that he left her on the dresser.

Mog was himself again, only this time he was relaxed, ready and eager to take on the world that was his for the taking. Mog was back! Let the humans beware!

CHAPTER TWO

A SIDEBAR NOTE FROM AUTHOR BUD SELIGSON

Before we continue with our narrative on the rise and fall of the Neanderthal nation (this can be correctly read as the rise and fall of "great leader Mog"), a few historical and important notes must be presented here. If a historical novelist, like myself, were to invent such a character as the real-life "Mog the Neanderthal," he would be accused of fantasy.

Born into a poor Neanderthal family of ancient lineage, Mog had no formal schooling, but yet, due to his unusual intelligence and great brute strength, he had the necessary qualities which lifted him up so rapidly and so spectacularly to the commanding heights of power as illustrated in the first book of this series, *ATIA: Bronze Age Warrior.*

Mog was gifted with a great leader's single-mindedness of purpose, ruthlessness, a remarkable capacity for sustained hard work, and above all, a strange and indefinable magnetism of personality, which nowadays would be described, inaccurately but vividly, as charisma.

Many of history's great leaders got by with only one of these great qualities. Some of them possessed two or more in varying degrees, but Mog had them all.

To study his life and his campaigns against his human enemies would be something like watching the operation of today's computers, programmed to give us information on the best of Neanderthal management or Neanderthal relations. Without a doubt, the name of Mog the Neanderthal would be printed out.

Mog's capacity for work was phenomenal. He appeared to have made do with four or five hours of sleep each night, and he was more than capable of dictating simultaneously to several members of his general staff and going from one subject to another without losing his train of thought on any of them.

In the matter of charisma, it would seem churlish to doubt the powers of this Neanderthal, who, in spite of his somewhat unpromising physical appearance, succeeded in enchanting successfully all those around him, whether male or female, human or Neanderthal.

Mog, as is often the fate of giants, has been the target of constant verbal attacks by others. He has been accused of insensitivity, bad manners, and vindictive cruelty— and it has to be conceded that he was often guilty of all of these. But no one who knows the real history of the human-Neanderthal wars has ever denied that Mog was a military genius and peerless leader of his people. His place in history is secure, and the story of his life makes irresistible reading.

And now our final note before we "get on with" the following concluding part of our trilogy

BUD'S CONCLUSION ON MOG THE NEANDERTHAL.

All in all, the Neanderthal army became a formidable weapon for Mog's limitless ambitions, as indeed, did the Neanderthal nation that he ultimately controlled and dominated. Mog was a heroic career soldier if one looks at everything from an unbiased viewpoint.

His career, which some would say was an excellent one, with which others would violently disagree, transformed the world he lived in and dominated for so many years. The implications of his achievements were profound, casting their shadows far into succeeding generations and leaving the Mog legend itself to be debated by successive schools of historians who were alternatively captivated or repelled by the sheer scale of his influence.

Mog should not be judged solely as a commander or as a national leader, or even as a contemporary Neanderthal who lived and resisted his own aggressiveness during his lifetime. He was one of those individuals whose lives have to be seen as part of history itself, shaped by the evolution of society and ideas both human and Neanderthal.

Mog's impact on contemporaries who witnessed at first hand the brilliance of his rise, the finality of his eclipse, and finally his death should not be ignored. Mog, the Neanderthal should live on in our collective memory. I know that he lives on in my own thoughts.
—Bud Seligson

CHAPTER THREE

The meeting was being held in one of those places that the humans had kept absolutely secret. It
was being held in one of those high and out-of-
the-way mountain retreats that could easily be secured
from the enemy. The meeting was called for by Supreme
Leader Atia, and he scheduled it so that enough time had
passed for things to calm down after the disaster brought
down on all of them by the clever Neanderthal leader.

Mog had taken a one-hundred-percent-certain
defeat and turned it completely around into a victory for
his makeshift army. Even though he had the lesser of the
two armies, and had inferior weapons, both large and
small, Mog had pulled absolute magic out of his large
Neanderthal hat once again and come out the winner,
and there was nothing that Atia or the rest of the generals
could do about it.

Sitting around the large table with Atia and talking
quietly to themselves were his son Anoti and all the
generals of the various armed forces. It has to be noted
that there were only three generals present because the
fourth general was sitting in the stockade, having been

found out as the spy in their midst who had given Mog inside information.

Atia had moved the generals around and the three remaining each had a different branch of the army under their command. Atia thought that it would be much better if they restarted their planning with a new person in charge of each of the three divisions. General Tukk was now in charge of the footsoldiers, General Ladd, of the archery divisions, and General Mann had the horse soldiers under his command. The original fourth general was now spending his days in complete isolation inside the deepest part of the holding stockade.

Atia opened up the meeting by reviewing the painful scene that they all had witnessed on the battlefield. Not one Neanderthal had been killed or wounded or even fired upon, while the human forces suffered losses of hundreds of fleeing soldiers, along with the trapped females who were the helpless pawns in all of this as they were murdered right there in front of everyone.

There was terrible anger among all the surviving humans, both male and female, as to what had been done to them all, and revenge was now on everyone's mind and in everyone's conversation. It was also very much on the mind of those who were sitting in on this strategy meeting. The only difference was that these men were cool, calm and calculating. Each of them knew that even though they had all suffered a terrible defeat at the hand of their enemy, it was just a matter of time and better planning before the Neanderthals would see what they all could do.

As they went around the room, each general was called upon to make suggestions, but not one idea could get them all to agree until they heard the plan laid out before them by the tricky and wise Supreme Leader. It was Atia' s wily plan that they all were able to support and embrace, and one that had a very good chance of working.

Atia made the point that their soldiers were not defeated in war, nor even in a simple battle. They only lost because of one person who had out-thought them all, and that person was Supreme Neanderthal Leader Mog. It was Mog who figured out how to win the day and it was Mog who they had to destroy. Without him, the Neanderthals would go back to fighting in small groups that could be easily defeated by the humans.

Without Mog, there would be no central planning and no smooth armed forces coming up against them. Without Mog, the world could be rid of the terrible wandering tribes of Neanderthals. Without Mog, the human armies could wipe out the Neanderthals no matter where they ran to. Without Mog, life would be wonderful!

Before he gave them the details of his plan to rid them once and for all of Mog, Atia spoke the sentence that would be repeated for many generations to come: "CUT OFF THE HEAD, AND THE BODY DIES WITH IT!"

CHAPTER FOUR

There was absolute silence in the room as each of the Generals and the son of Atia looked at each other as they turned their attention back to their Supreme Leader.

Atia was now standing center stage facing them all with a grim smile on his face. "I believe we all agree that with Mog alive and doing his amazing things with the Neanderthals, it would be almost impossible for us to root out and completely destroy the Neanderthal threat to all of us.

"The things that I am going to tell you now must never leave this room. Each of us has proven their loyalty and devotion to the cause of defeating the Neanderthal and making the world safe for humankind. And I must caution you that if this plan fails, there will be no other thoughts or ideas out there for us to follow, and humans will be doomed.

"If what I am about to tell you does not work, I am afraid that the human race as we know it will vanish from the Earth, and what will be left will be our deaths, destruction, and slavery for those who follow us."

When the noise level from everyone in the room talking at the same time finally quieted down, Atia began his narrative. In a quiet but firm voice that carried well throughout the large meeting room, he told them that from time to time there were enemies of the human nation who had mixed loyalties and quite often would secretly aid the Neanderthal cause.

Whenever a name and evidence was brought up before him at one of the many security meetings, he would have the charges investigated quietly and in great detail. Most of the reports that crossed his desk were found out to be mistaken and merely expressions of anger and/or envy on the part of the persons filing the complaint. However, when the facts given to him proved to be true, and a traitor of Neanderthal loyalty was revealed, he always personally got involved in the case and decided one way or the other on the innocence or guilt of the named person.

The latest and most current case that he gave as an example was that of General Zamath, who was now locked up in the stockade. It was General Zamath who had sent messages to Mog that gave him inside information on all of them, their weapons, and their plans. It was General Zarnath who gave Mog information and the time he needed to come up with his counter-moves against them that were so successful.

"Under the threat of his losing his life, the general told us how he would have one of his men fire an arrow into the compound where Mog would be staying. Attached to the arrow was a letter with all names, plans, new weapons, and movements of our people. With this advanced knowledge, we now know in hind sight, how the disaster that just happened to us came about.

"Here is my proposal," a now-smiling Atia quietly said.

"Let us take a page out of the planning book of Mog the Neanderthal and use his own cleverness against him.

"Mog does not know that we have his spy, General Zarnath, locked up. The plan is to keep on sending the monthly arrow messages to him, only this time we will tell him what we want him to know as we sign Zarnath's name. By playing things this way, we will be turning Mog's inside information against him and feeding him false and misleading information.

"And this takes us to the second part of my plan, which is the most dangerous part of all. I have a plan of how to kill Supreme Leader Mog, and do it in such a manner that the Neanderthals will never know that his death was caused by us. And here is how it will be done."

There was not a sound in the entire room as Supreme Leader Atia outlined his plan to rid the known world of its greatest danger—Mog, the Neanderthal.

CHAPTER FIVE

His first name was Jam and his last name was Ess. Together he was called James.

James was an assassin. And he was usually available for hire. For a large payment in gold or silver coin, he would carry out an assassination with style and deadly results. James did not work very often but when he did he was dedicated to his profession, and tried to perform his contracted obligations with class, style and professionalism.

James was a special twenty-three-year-old male who stood five foot nine inches tall and weighed in at a muscular one hundred and eighty pounds. He was nice-looking, with dark wavy hair, and was always successful with the ladies since he always had plenty of coin to spend on them.

The term was not yet part of the human language in these early years but we would call James a hit man, who would work for the supreme leader, Atia, when called upon. He also did his own things as a killer for hire when the target was someone that he thought needed killing.

James did his own work and made a very nice living

for himself, but he had high standards and would only kill for hire after he carefully investigated the potential target to make sure that a killing was in order. He would turn down many offers for his services if he did not agree that taking a man's life was the right thing to do for one good reason or another. James would never accept an assignment to kill a female. They were untouchable in his mind, and he left dealing with them to others who did not have his high morals.

James was skilled with every type of personal weapon that was available. Knives (his favorite for up-close and personal use), swords (for an open-ended, out-in-the-open duel), bow and arrow for assassination at a distance (when he could not get close enough for knife or sword), and spear when his target was getting away.

Right at this moment we find James relaxing after completing a private contract that had him moving about the countryside in order to locate his agreed-upon target.

He was out on assignment, having been well paid in advance to remove an evil highway man who would rob, kill and rape whenever he came across humans who ventured out into the surrounding wilderness.

James, having completed his assignment, was relaxing in one of the local bath houses where we catch up with him in a relaxed and pleasant mood.

IC Э<Œ

A cloud of steam rose as the girl poured another bucket of boiling water into the bath water.
James, wedged into the wooden tub and unable to evade the almost scalding water, cursed with his mouth full of

wine, and swatted at the wench with the chicken carcass he held in his other hand.

The girl,—James had already forgotten her name— laughed coarsely, and knelt to scrub his back with a sponge and sulfurous-smelling soap.

James did notice that her thin cotton shift, wet and clinging to her body, outlined a very substantial physique which had his full attention. James, a tankard of wine in one fist, and a half-cooked chicken in the other, suffered her ministrations with aplomb.

After cleaning up from the dust and dirt that he had accumulated on the way into the small settlement and paying the girl well for her services, James allowed himself to be led to the local swordsmith arcade where hand weapons of all sizes and types were available for purchase.

He had lost his sword in his hasty flight away from a wandering band of Neanderthals that had picked up and then lost his trail in the wooded areas not far from the compound he had fled to.

James had a deep-rooted hatred for all things Neanderthal but did not push himself to fight them as yet. One day when the war that his friend and Supreme Leader Atia was always talking about finally arrived, James knew that he would be among the first to volunteer in the fight against the hated beast-men. Until that day arrived, he had decided to keep well away from the dangerous wandering bands of killers.

There were several broadswords in the storeroom, and the one that caught his eye had a finely sharped edge on its watered-steel blade. He knew that such blades as this one were rare and quite uncommon in an outpost stockade like this.

He really liked this blade, he decided. It was a very fine weapon, wide, single-bladed, with a basket handle and a complex hand guard of loops and shells.

The watering of the blade showed that it was dipped in the forge-fire when it was made, several times to add to its strength. He could see an infinite number of water marks on it which he knew would serve him well as a weapon when it struck other weapons. It should be able to destroy any other weapon upon hard contact.

The seller of weapons, named Hut, was telling James that he personally preferred the rapier (straight and narrow sword) to the wide dueling blade that James had selected.

Hut went on to say that the rapier is a lighter, nimbler blade that gives you a longer reach in fencing, and has an edge for slashing and a sharp point for a direct thrust.

"I disagree with your choice," said a smiling James.

"I've seen a drunken soldier take a rapier thrust through his chest and keep on fighting until he cut his killer in half and killed two of his other enemies before he stumbled over a bench and died of his wounds."

"I like more fire-power in my blade, and being as tall as I am, I can easily swing a large blade of this size. Give me a strong blade like this with a good edge on it, and I'll cut my way out of any trouble that I might find myself in."

"Of course, you are right," said the seller of weapons as he took the two large gold coins that James handed him for the purchase. "And I wish you well with your new blade."

CHAPTER SIX

Early dawn was almost upon him as the sky started to clear and the last of the bright stars in the sky began to fade. The season had changed from summer to autumn and it was pleasant to see the turn of the year from summer's dry heat to the autumn's cool explosions of color all around.

James walked along the path between the clear sparkling water of the grassy river banks and the black-streaked white limestone cliffs. He was following the narrow trail that led into the beginning of Neanderthal territory, and all his senses were alert for any dangers that might be offered up to him. Just ahead was a smaller path that had been described to him as a more direct route toward the crossing place where the flowing water spread out and became shallow and easily passed over.

James had a meeting set up with one of Atia's special field agents who would guide him through the defensive lines that the Neanderthals had set up to keep humans away from their territory and away from seeing what they were doing with their plans for the extermination of all humanity.

He crossed over the described double-peaked small hilly range of low mountains and headed across a flat field toward the meeting place where he knew that he needed to go. James never looked back from where he came from as he continued to walk along the faint pathway.

It was his way to always go forward, because he did not want to think about the grief and anger that was always with him in this terrible world that humans and Neanderthals shared. When he thought about his many friends and family that had lost their lives to the beast-men, he felt squeezed by the grip of raw intense and unsettling emotions that made him want to kill and destroy the enemy.

He knew that he needed to clear his head for the mission that he knew the supreme leader was going to give him. Atia had always said that when the time was right James was going to be his strong right hand for the destruction of the enemy.

The message he had received a few days ago, along with the directions to Atia's field camp, caused James to drop what he was doing and prepare himself for whatever was asked of him. After the terrible defeat of the humans at the hands of the Neanderthals in the field of battle, James thought that it was only a matter of time before he would be summoned. Whatever it was that Atia asked of him, he was prepared to do.

He had long ago realized that his life would be forfeit to the needs of the mission that Atia would send him on, and he was prepared to give up his own life if events came down to this. All he needed to do now was to find his guide for the final leg of his journey to meet up in the field with his friend and supreme leader Atia.

All of his life, James had had a tendency to overreact to events that were going on around him. Overreacting seemed to run in his family, and this was what had caused the death of his father and all his uncles. It was something that he wanted to avoid at all costs. He wanted to think of himself as a thinking man. A full-scale frontal attack to one's problems might be fine if you knew what you were up against. But if he was going to go up against something extraordinary like this Mog thing, then caution and planning seemed to be the way to go.

With all these good intentions in mind, he finally arrived at the meeting site, where he saw his guide waiting with horses to take them on their continued journey to the hidden camp of Atia.

༄ ༅ ༆

They finally arrived at the camp site and were able to dismount and walk the final distance to the camp itself. The camp had the pleasant smell of men and horses all mingled together.

CHAPTER SEVEN

J ames could clearly smell the wood smoke, roasting meat, leather and oil, all intermingled in the firelight where the men talked, sharpened weapons, repaired gear, ate, gambled, slept, drank and with eager eyes watched my guide and I walk up to the midst of a trio of tattered tents, where we were asked to stop.

A tense atmosphere of silence expanded around us as we stopped and looked around.

We paused before the second-largest tent, and my guide spoke with a soldier who was moving in the direction of the larger tent off to our right.

Their exchange lasted for several minutes, and then our guard walked over to the main tent and spoke with someone there for a minute or two.

He came back and approached me. "The officers are all at a meeting with the Supreme Leader in the general tent. Set your things down over there. It will be a while until Atia will be able to see you. I will graze your horse and put him up for the night. Please help yourself to some food and drink at any of the nearby fires."

James nodded and set about stowing his belongings

and getting some dinner. He did not realize how hungry he was until he started eating beside one of the fires.

After what was probably an hour and a half, the shadows stirred within the large tent that he was watching. It was several minutes after that before the entrance cover was thrown aside, and men began to emerge, slowly, talking among themselves, glancing back within. The last two tarried at the threshold, still talking with someone who remained inside. The rest of them passed outside and went toward the other tents. The two at the entrance edged their way outside, still facing the interior.

James could hear the sound of their voices, although he could not make out what was being said. As they drifted farther outside, the man with whom they were all speaking moved also, and James caught a glimpse of him. The light was at his back, and the two officers blocked most of James' view, but he could still see that he was thin and quite tall.

James continued to stare, willing them to move farther away from the opening so that he would have a better look at the man for whom he had traveled all this way to see. The man that he knew to be Atia.

Atia finally stepped outside then, and a breeze caught the cloak he wore and caused it to flare to his right. James saw that his shirt was yellow, his trousers brown, and the cloak itself was a flame-like orange. He caught the edge of the cloak with a rapid movement of his left hand and drew it back.

James stood up quickly, and the leaders' head snapped in his direction. Their gazes met, and neither of them moved for several heartbeats after that.

The two officers turned and stared, and then Atia

pushed them aside and was striding toward James. He halted several paces before James, and his hazel eyes swept over him.

Atia seldom smiled, but he managed a faint one this time. "Come with me," he said as he turned back toward his large tent. James followed him, leaving his gear where it lay.

Atia dismissed the two officers with a glance and motioned him in. He followed and let the flap fall behind him. James' eyes took in a bedroll, a small table, benches, weapons and a campaign chest.

Atia clasped James' s hands and smiled again. "Son of a bitch!" he said with a huge smile on his face. "My wandering nephew has finally come back to me."

"Uncle Atia, I see that you are also still alive. It is wonderful to see you. It has been too many years since I saw you last."

CHAPTER EIGHT

The human-Neanderthal female dancer Suzy's appearance at the huge arena excited comments from everyone in the overflowing crowd of Neanderthals who were there to celebrate Supreme Leader Mog's exciting victory over the humans on the battlefield earlier in the month. An unbelievable story was going around about how Mog had outsmarted them and won the day without losing one soldier in the field.

Mog was being hailed as the nearest thing to a god that the Neanderthals could ever believe in. There never was anyone like him before, and there might never be anyone like him again. He was riding at the top of his popularity, and he was loving it.

He was especially excited amid the naked debauchery going on around him as the evening's entertainment was about to begin. Of course, he was sitting front and center and extremely low down in the best box seat at the stadium.

He had wonderful memories of this special stadium. This was where he had originally moved himself up the leadership ladder of the armed forces by removing his enemies in wrestling matches to the death and a fantastic sword fight ending in the death of his female human opponent that had absolutely everyone talking about him for the very first time.

Tonight, he was invited here by the stadium management to see the famous human-Neanderthal female dancer perform for him and the rest of the nation for the first time. The talk going on around him about her was that her dancing was unbelievable and was a once-in-a-lifetime show.

Mog was very pleased and excited with the things going on as he waved his hand to all of his admiring fans.

When Suzy entered the huge stadium's raised platform, the crowd went wild as she simply stood there, soaking up the atmosphere being created by her presence. As she stood still, everyone began to quiet down until they all were looking down upon her supple dancer's figure hidden beneath the fluttering streamers of her brightly colored feathered cloak.

A special meeting was arranged for after the dance, when Mog would have the honor of having her come to his private compound for dinner, some conversation, and hopefully some fooling around. It was all very exciting, and Mog had cleaned himself up until his appearance was more than acceptable.

It was a very special event for anyone to have a private evening with the world-famous dancer, but then, Mog knew that he was just not anyone.

He was Mog!

He deserved every honor and every privilege that he received.

The stadium broke into an absolute silence as everyone just sat there quietly and watched Suzy walk across the hard-packed entertainment area and speak briefly with her backup musicians. She had made all the necessary arrangements with them earlier in the day, and she was just reviewing all the instructions.

Within a few minutes, Suzy walked away from them and took her position on center stage as the string instruments, flutes and drums went into a quick, trilling melody.

Mog, watching everything that was going on, knew little if anything about music. He didn't recognize the musical piece that they were playing, but the rest of the growing audience made a bright chatter of applause.

Suzy stood in the center of the raised circle. She made a fantastic figure of a female who stood perfectly still as she waited for every eye to feast upon the sight of her. Her feathered cape continued to completely envelop her from her neck to her ankles as she paused there motionless. Behind the falcon mask that entirely enclosed her face, her glowing eyes stared out at the audience without blinking as she intentionally positioned herself to give Supreme Leader Mog the best view of herself. Suzy had several special requests that she planned to ask Mog to grant her, and there was no better way to get what she wanted from him than to show off what his reward would be if he went along with her wants and desires.

Suzy suddenly leaped up, throwing her arms outward in a gesture aimed directly at the great leader, and the crowd went wild as Mog just sat there admiring what his special dessert for the evening was going to be.

Her arms rose outward in a gesture that lifted her

covering cloak from her sides like the spreading wings of a bird taking flight. For a moment, she seemed to hang suspended in mid-air, with her generously endowed slim figure completely naked, as she gently settled back to the waiting ground beneath her delicate feet. Then, even as their breath caught in hundreds of watching throats, she fell lightly to the floor, her nudity still concealed by the flurry of feathers.

Across the dark floor, Susy danced—now sweeping low or spinning gracefully in a full circle, then rising into the air in sudden and very graceful leaps of her muscular legs. So swift were her movements that the wreaths of white and umber feathers swirled all about her like living wings—one moment revealing a blur of her white, well-formed breasts or a highly tanned thigh.

The musicians increased the tempo of the melody, and Suzy seemed to fly above the hard-packed dirt floor. She was simply amazing as she soared, darting this way and that as she rose up and dived down. Her audience, including Supreme Leader Mog, was completely caught up in the swiftly moving female body as it made its sensational moves on stage.

The audience, still vividly remembering the first leaping vision of her naked beauty, watched entranced as the flurry of her cloak enticed their eyes with the instantaneous disclosing and veiling of the dancer's charms. Faster and faster the tempo of her dancing increased! It was only a well-trained danseuse who could maintain such a pace and have mastered the intricate gestures and movements that went along with it.

Many of the watchers were beginning to speculate as to what the face hidden beneath the mask looked like.

And finally, at long last as the frenetic music reached

a crescendo, Suzy once again leapt high into the air with her arms outstretched. Her cloak of feathers spun straight out and away from her shoulders, disclosing her entire figure in nude perfection, as she seemed to take flight above the floor.

Suzy made an exaggerated low bow to her audience and to her special guest, Mog. She then turned and disappeared into the welcoming hands of her handmaidens as they bundled her up and led her away.

CHAPTER NINE

Several hours had passed since Suzy had been whisked away by her bodyguards from the arena where she had more than entertained the huge crowd.

Mog had no problem leaving the area since almost everyone completely ignored him. They were all still thinking about the unbelievingly sexy dance that they had just witnessed.

Mog was not happy being ignored and thought about what punishment he could give to Suzy for taking away his moment of glory at the arena. Mog had been really looking forward to all the attention that Suzy received that he thought should have been his. He was not happy with Suzy even before he met her.

However, Mog calmed himself down about the Suzy thing when he thought that soon he would have her all to himself in his own private quarters, and he could do to her whatever he wanted to do to her while she was there with him. It was good to be the king in his own castle, and he was happy about that,

He was also thinking about that sexy body all

wrapped up in feathers and not much else as he moved about his personal living quarters, putting everything in place so as to give a good impression of the field office that he called home when he was away from the city. He was expecting Suzy within a very short while, and he moved things around as he cleaned the place up a bit.

⟨⟩ ⟨⟩ ⟨⟩

Her name was Suzy—just Suzy—and he thought that this was interesting since his name was Mog—just Mog.

From the very first moment when she entered his living quarters, he knew that he absolutely hated her! She was everything he disliked in a female. She was overbearing and had to be in charge of everything, and nothing he showed her or offered her was good enough. He grew a dislike of her almost instantly.

The only good thing that he did like about her was her great body. She was slim like a human female but had the oversized Neanderthal breasts that he loved so much.

He decided that he would listen to her complaints and her suggestions and to what else she wanted from him. He would do this in order to have the wild sex orgy that he promised himself she would have to give him if she wished to walk away and not be carried away.

CHAPTER TEN

Mog raised his head from her thighs and licked the entire area with a big smile on his ugly face. "More?" he said, with a sadistic grin going from ear to ear.

Suzy, gasping for breath and trembling with aftershocks from the violent love-making, responded, "Oh, yes! More would be wonderful!"

She continued her chatter that was driving Mog crazy. He was thinking that she would never stop talking. He hated talkative woman, but he would put up with this one for a little while longer. The sex was absolutely wonderful and he could ignore her non-stop talking if he had to.

Suzy was still talking while taking in all that Mog was giving to her. "I don't think that I have ever responded to anyone making love to me as I have to you. You are quite the great lover; Supreme Leader Mog!"

A smiling Mog whispered softly, "I am so glad to have pleased you so far, my dear young lady." He rose from between her spread thighs and crawled up a bit to stare into her eyes with his face barely an inch away from hers, while his mouth descended once again upon hers.

She opened up for his kiss as his teeth gently scored upon her lips and scratched the tender flesh inside her cheeks. A sweet copper taste flavored her tongue. It was the taste of blood—her blood—and a tiny illicit thrill raced up and down her spine.

While straddling her thighs with his knees down on the huge mattress, Mog caught her legs, which were pressed back against the mattress, and easily lifted her legs up and onto his shoulder, spreading her wide. Then he turned her hips to the side.

Suzy had to arch her back and throw her arms out for balance. "Just what the hell are you doing, Mog?"

Mog paused for a moment, spreading his knees wide as his love-tool, a thick, long and very rigid curve, pressed against the entrance to her body once again.

"What am I doing? How could you ask that at this moment? I am making love to you, woman, and I am going about it in my own personal Mog style!"

Suzy swallowed. He looked awfully big to her. "Take it easy there, Mog. I'm not too big where you are going."

Mog smiled, and it was a pure self-satisfied male smile. "I will fit," he said simply.

Suzy was still very moist internally from their previous sexual encounter, and he slid in quickly, deeply, taking her to the full extent of her depth with one great lunge.

They both gasped at the same time.

Suzy stopped the beginning of a groan as she felt her internal organs stretch themselves to accommodate him. She had no idea how the hell she was able to hold him in her, but she had—and it was quite an accomplishment.

Mog pulled back a bit with a slight moan of his own. *You were right, Suzy. You were nice and tight but you won't be that way when I get done with you!*

Suzy arched under him as pleasure built up with a simmering heat that rose and held at just this side of boiling. Each of his strong thrusts struck against something internally that made her jolt and clench with each entry. It did feel incredibly good, but she suddenly felt that he was going about it way too slow. She tried to shift under him but he was too heavy for her to move him.

"Faster!" she cried, but he ignored her and kept moving at his own steady pace.

Mog smiled down at her as he told her that he was afraid that he would finish much sooner than he wanted to, if he picked up the pace. He said that he needed to maintain a slow, steady series of moves, and that she would have to stay with him on it. He smiled as he said to her that he didn't see where she had any choice in the matter.

"Besides," he said, "you must have noticed by now that it is you on the bottom and me on top. Top person calls the shots and you are definitely not the top person here!"

Mog reached up and caught her around her neck, pulling her breast down to his open mouth. His other hand cupped her rear end, his fingers digging into the soft plump flesh. His mouth made enthusiastic wet sounds as he suckled hard on her breast and pounded up and into her with hard swift thrusts.

"Oh, yes, yes!" Suzy cried out, gasping with delight, her slim body strained to match his now-increased pounding rhythm. "YES, YES, LOVE ME MOG, LOVE ME!"

His climax coiled and tightened into white-hot sensations. Shivers danced up and down Suzy's spine as she neared another climax and then another!!

Mog growled, a low and liquid rumbling deep from within his mighty chest. His arms were locked around her neck as he once again pulled her breast against his wide-open mouth.

His teeth pressed into the soft flesh around the pale areola of her nipple, and it hurt her! Fear suddenly struck Suzy as she began to think that she was making love to a madman who would never stop. As her fear raced through her, and her climax rose within her to a vicious crescendo, she began to twist herself away from him, but she couldn't move away. His body weight was still too much for her.

His gaze was hard and even cruel-looking as he looked down on her, while his tongue swirled across the still-taut flesh surrounding her nipple. His arms tightened and his fingers knotted in her hair, holding her completely helpless as he went into the final stages of completing his own personal sex act.

Another climax of Suzy's exploded within her in a violent, skull-burning rush of rapture, ripping screams of terror and joy from her throat at the very same time.

Mog howled and bucked in her arms, driven to the edge of sanity by the horrific power of the dark and brutal rush that he forced upon them both.

Overwhelmed by the sheer power of her final climax, she collapsed in his arms, barely conscious and straining to catch her breath.

The Neanderthal eased her over onto her side, pressing her against the back of the mattress once again. He was almost purring with happiness as he grasped her neck in a strong grip with both hands and twisted until he heard the satisfying sound of her neck breaking.

He carefully climbed off of the now-dead female, proceeded to wash himself up with a nearby pan of water, got dressed, called the waiting guard outside to clean up and dispose of the body, and then calmly walked out of the room and went on his way.

He was Mog! He could be heard to be humming a little tune as he slowly strolled down the partially lighted path.

CHAPTER ELEVEN

Atia was quietly sitting there with James as the two men were enjoying each other's company. Atia was remembering the violent action on the battlefield with his nephew for the first time, when they had suddenly found themselves surrounded by a band of Neanderthals. This was the first-time James had been battle-tested, and it was most impressive.

Some men are said to have been born for the battlefield, but James had actually been born *on* the field of battle, as his warrior mother had delivered him while an actual fight was going on around them. The smells drawn in with his first breath of life had been those of blood and death, and the first sounds he heard were those of the clash of bronze and steel swords. The first sights his eyes beheld had been ravens, circling the sky, waiting until the living men and women departed and they could descend and rule over what remained down below.

And so, with the battle fury that had been his birthright, James strode through the flames and screams of the encampment and it was death itself that rode on his naked sword-arm. He sought out the semi-naked Neanderthals, and with his weapon of choice in his right hand, made the enemy's last memory of the world of mankind, one of blood and steel—their blood and his steel!

His trusty broadsword flashed banefully in the light of the fires, flashed until its bloodied length could flash no more. Neanderthals faced him, and Neanderthals fell before him, and at last no enemy was left to oppose him. The time came shortly when he stood alone, and no enemy could his questing eye find but those of the dead.

This was the first time, and now James came to report to his commander-in-chief about the last assignment Atia had given him. It was an impossible assignment, but James took it for love of his uncle.

"Report," said Atia, as the two of them relaxed for the moment before the warming fire that blazed in the leaders' tent.

Iᑕ Ǝᐊ(Ǝ

In a soft voice that was just above a loud whisper, James began his report, picking his words most carefully.

James was not a happy man as he began speaking. "I was as hard as stone and as dark as the soil that I walked on. I was as mean as hell and I was on a worthy mission. Today would be the day. I donned my visor, put on my best clothes, and hung my double-bladed sword at my side. Then I fastened my cloak at my neck with a silver buckle once given to me by my uncle Atia, the supreme leader of all the forces fighting to free the world of that evil embodied by the Neanderthals.

"My men and I were on a special mission about a mile and a half inside of the territory that was held by the

Neanderthals when their attack began. There were five hundred of us, all armed and mounted on horseback as we encountered about an equal number of Neanderthals who were on foot.

"After bitter fighting that seemed to go on for hours, we broke their ranks and they all turned and disappeared into the nearby forest. Our numbers had dwindled down from the original five hundred to just a little over three hundred as we slowly continued moving forward toward our destination.

"A few hours later, after we had stopped by a nearby running stream of water and eaten, sharpened our weapons, and watered the horses, we once again mounted and continued moving forward.

"A thin line of Neanderthal foot soldiers, carrying their huge spears, barred our way. They stood there waiting for us stoically as we slowly bore down on them. We charged, and the fighting began in earnest, and shortly our numbers had dwindled down to a little above two hundred as we again moved forward.

"We topped a rise, and far ahead and below us lay a dark series of low-lying tents and campfires. I raised my blade and signaled an attack as we descended down upon the waiting enemy.

"When the battle ended, the now-one hundred and fifty of us stormed ahead as the Neanderthals fell by the wayside, and we swept past them. We reached the gate to their outpost, which was our intended target, as the beast-men met our charge head-on. They outnumbered us now, but we had little choice but to keep moving forward. To stop or retreat meant certain death and defeat, and so we continued moving forward toward our destination.

"We slew and we slew until our arms were beyond weary and finally the enemy faded away in the late afternoon sunlight. We had won through, and then there were only a few dozen enemy soldiers standing in our way, and the fifty or so of us that remained made short work of them."

James turned away from the skirmish that was going on around him and raced to the rear of the structure, away from the battle. He came to a heavy wooden door at the entrance to the series of rooms. He tried to open it but it was secured from the other side, so he kicked it as hard as he could, and it fell inward with a crash.

James saw Leader Mog just standing there quietly, looking at a map of sorts. He saw a man-formed huge body, dressed in light armor, with a big ugly head resting upon massive shoulders. James crossed the threshold and stopped.

Mog had turned to stare at the fallen door and then he sought to find my eyes through the face cover that I was wearing. "Human man, you have come too far," he said, and suddenly his blade leaped into his hand.

There were footsteps on the stairs behind me as I stepped to the side to allow them to enter. Several of my men burst in and stopped perfectly still as they saw Mog and me just standing there with our swords drawn, taking up a defensive dueling position.

I expected Mog to step forward and fight me, one on one, to see who was the better man, but once again the smart and wily Mog did the unexpected, which saved his life.

He did what any experienced sword-fighter would never do, because it was a foolish move on his part.

He hurled his blade at me, point forward, and I barely blocked it, as I did not expect such a move.

In the several moments it took me to recover from blocking his thrown sword, Mog crashed headlong into the closed set of double windows and fell to the ground below. In mere moments, he was out of sight as he faded away into the darkness. I held back my men, knowing that to send them after him in the dark would be sending them out to die.

Mog had done it again! He had escaped once more to continue his fight against the entire human race. I had failed in my mission, and Mog, the greatest enemy of mankind, would continue to plague us all.

In failure and dejection, I led my few remaining companions out of Neanderthal territory and back to our camp, where I am now reporting my mission's failure.

CHAPTER TWELVE

Icy air hung deadly still among the crags of the tall mountain peaks. This was quite normal for the Alps, mountains located on the border of modern-day Italy and its neighbor to the south.

This most secret of locations was deep within the very heart of the arm of those mountains that stretched south and west along the running border of human/ Neanderthal territories.

No bird sang, and the cloudless azure sky was empty, for even the always-present vultures could find no moving air currents upon which to soar.

The tall, gray-eyed thirty-nine-year-old Supreme Leader Atia, along with his son Anoti, were slowly winding their way to the special place where this most important of meetings was going to take place in the very early morning hours of the new day. After the failure of the attempt to assassinate Mog at his temporary headquarters away from his usually well-protected army fortifications, a frustrated Atia had called this meeting to bring together the best minds of all humanity to come up with a new and better plan.

They had once again underestimated the clever-thinking Neanderthal leader! Mog had once again been able to laugh at their feeble attempts to defeat him. The terrible shame of it all was quite evident, causing Supreme Leader Atia to call together the very best of all of humanity's leaders.

Atia called this a Special Summit Meeting, and it was to be the next and hopefully final step in the attempt to rid themselves of the clever Supreme Leader Mog once and for all. There was no discussion upon the point that Mog had to be eliminated, or else there would be no place for humanity to flee to. The Neanderthals would come after them one by one until humans would be only a footnote to Neanderthal historical memories. The humans knew that they were correct in believing that without Mog to lead them, the Neanderthals would soon fall apart and revert back to their original tribes once more, and would thereby be easier to defeat one tribe at a time.

Atia was looking forward to seeing his old friend and bodyguard, X, and X's daughter once again. He owed his very life to X, who had saved him from a personal attack by Mog. That terrible attack, which had almost killed him, gave Atia a little bit of an insight into the mind of his mortal enemy.

Up to and until that moment, Mog was an unknown personality, and it was most difficult to deal with the unknown. But even in the brief conversation that he had with Mog just before Mog attacked him within the human compound, Atia found out that he was not dealing with a supreme being. Mog, he found out in those few moments, was just as intelligent as the clever minds of the human leaders. His intelligence was high, but he made mistakes just like they all did, and had no special mental thinking process beyond that of a human.

Atia believed that he could put himself mentally into Mog's place (in his shoes, so to speak, if he ever wore any) and think about what he would do if he was Mog. By sort of figuring out what he would do if he *was* Mog, Atia thought that, with the help of his staff, they could work out how Mog would act and react to situations as they came up. He was feeling confident for the first time in many days about all this.

And another factor was racing back and forth in his mind as he rode slowly toward his destination. It was his latest talk with his wife, Ava.

Ava, whom he always treated as an equal, but someone who had to be specially sheltered from the hard decisions of his life as leader of the Armed Forces, came up with something wonderful to add to the mix. Women, wives, lovers, both young and old, would no longer be satisfied staying at home and waiting for news about what was happening out there in the violent world away from their sheltered lives! They demanded that, and would not be satisfied until, they also were included in the day-to-day fight against the hated enemy. They would no longer be stay-at-home females! They demanded that they be weapons-trained, and soldier-trained, and riders of horses—and whatever their men, sons and lovers could do, they demanded that they be taught to do the same.

Atia, with Ava's partnership, was beginning to form an all-female army and cavalry and supply and combat units, that would train and fight alongside their male counterparts.

Even as Atia left on this journey with Anoti to meet up with other leaders, Ava was busy training and expanding the fighting forces of humanity, and the reports that he was receiving from some of the male training officers were that the females were fiercer, more deadly and more willing to fight and die for the cause then were the regular armed forces. They were becoming a new—and possibly the greatest—weapon that the humans had ever had, and females from all over the known human world were flocking to join the fight. The size of the human fighting forces was increasing at a tremendous rate!

Atia smiled to himself when he thought that, even though Mog had won the last battle, he probably had lost his own war by his misuse of the human females as shields.

Atia smiled again when he thought of the many times he had a disagreement with Ava, and not only did she get in the last word in every disagreement, but she was usually right. Being right nine out of ten times was not something that he ever wanted to tell her, but these facts stuck in his head.

Women were the greatest thing that men had going for them, and if they could only figure out how to properly use them, he thought that the Neanderthals were doomed; it was as simple as that! The only problem was in just deciding what their next move would be, and that is why all the leaders would be gathered together in the morning.

With great excitement in his heart and mind, Atia continued to plod along on his slow-moving horse, heading for the meeting that could finally end the conflict forever.

CHAPTER THIRTEEN

James' life was leaking out of him in a dozen different places. He didn't think it was possible to lose so much blood and still be alive. He knew that he had only a few minutes left to live, probably less.

His fighting companions would find him by picking up his trail through the heavily wooded area, but they would not be in time to save him. He would definitely be dead within a very few minutes and there was no way that he could prevent it.

This new mission that he had undertaken would be his final one. It had been another mess right from the start, but this time he could not walk away as he had from the other disasters. James had no idea how the Neanderthals had caught on to him, and he would never know how his cover had been blown. But that issue was suddenly no longer of any consequence to him.

James realized that he personally did not matter anymore in the overall scheme of things, but what did matter was that he did not finish his assignment of taking the life of the leader of the Neanderthals. Supreme leader

Mog seemed to have a charmed life and no matter what situation that he found himself involved in, he would, one way or another, get himself out of harm's way.

But Mog had made a major mistake this time. In his hurry to flee, he had not looked at James to be sure that he was dead.

This was a major mistake only if James could hang on a little bit longer and transmit his special information to the supreme war council of the humans. His new information was vital, and if he could get it out, then his death would not be in vain. It mattered a great deal to him to get that information out so that he could get his dying revenge upon Mog, even from his own grave.

James was no longer feeling any pain. The only thing he now felt was a deep and numbing cold. His breath was coming in burbling gasps and he was shivering, even though it was a warm spring day. *A lovely time to die*, he thought, as he started coughing up blood.

He dragged himself slowly across the forest floor, leaving a wide trail of blood behind him as a way of marking a trail for his men to find him. With each movement, more of his intestines tumbled out onto the ground, but he did not bother to push them back into his body cavity. What was the point? He was a dead man anyway, and nothing mattered except what he had learned.

After what seemed like an eternity, he had dragged himself back to where he had hidden his small camp, and where the writing paper that he was after would be in easy reach. If only he had time enough to put his thoughts together and get his message down, and then be found by his men when they finally got to him.

His vision was suddenly getting blurred and he was

so very dizzy. He had never thought that it would end like this. It was so undignified to die cut up as he was.

His men would find him shortly and he would be dead, but hopefully his vital information would be gotten out and his uncle Atia would see that he had not died in vain.

He began to write on the tablet, using his own red blood as the necessary ink. There was a plentiful supply of this unusual liquid material.

He prayed to his personal god, Mars, who was the great god of war, to let him live long enough to write down his message. He needed just a few more minutes of time to do what he needed to do. *Time,* he thought to himself as he began to write out his message—*all things come down to time.*

When his men finally found him and his message written in blood, he was slumped against a tree with his eyes wide open, looking up at the sky in an unseeing stare. Completely surrounding them all was a beautiful spring morning, and the birds were in the nearby trees singing their hearts out with special songs of spring.

CHAPTER FOURTEEN

Atia took his position in the front of the large room and looked around at the assembled people, who were quietly talking among themselves.

Everyone seemed comfortable with each other since they had all know each other for a long time. There were however, a few new people present who easily fit into the ebb and flow of the soft conversations, and they were X's daughter Char, the secretary for Atia, who would keep notes upon what was said at the meeting, and Atia's new bodyguard Conan, who had become his shadow, coming and going everywhere that Atia went. Atia, who knew everyone and everything that was going on, was considered too valuable to allow him to be at risk again, and so the minute-to-minute bodyguard's presence became an accepted fact of daily life.

The room grew silent as each person became aware of Atia as he stood there waiting for their attention. In his own quiet way, Atia looked around the room as he smiled at everyone present. Anoti, his son, X, his former bodyguard and the man who saved his life, his daughter Char, who had recently brought them inside information on the thought process of Supreme Leader Mog, the generals of the foot soldiers, horse soldiers, and archers. And finally, his new bodyguard Conan and his note-taking secretary.

Atia reviewed how the disaster had happened when Mog had used captured human female slaves to turn the tide of battle in favor of his Neanderthals. He did not go into the details again because this was a terrible event that everyone was trying to put behind them.

He told them that they had arrested and locked up the traitor who was giving Mog inside information on new weapons, new formations and other most important goings-on that allowed Mog to win the battle. Before they went into their new planning to turn things around in their favor, he asked if everyone would read the copy of the note sent by the traitor to Mog that had allowed the events that followed it to happen. The note read as follows:

Hey Mog:

Here is my question to you!

The humans have made these slingshots by the thousands, and they are now part of the equipment that every human soldier has on his body at every moment.

So how will you stop this flying stone from killing every one of your soldiers?

I have no idea and maybe you should try and sign a peace treaty with the humans because I have to tell you now about the next secret weapon that they have come up with, called a ballista!

A ballista works just like the slingshot that you probably just held in your hand, only it is maybe a hundred times bigger. Believe me when I tell you that they can perfectly control it, and they can shoot hundreds of rocks, bits of iron and other things at your men, who will not have a chance against it!!!

Again, I suggest that maybe a peace treaty is your best way out of the mess that you are in.

There is no way to defeat these two weapons, and if you can find a way out, then you will be the absolute smartest Neanderthal or human that ever lived in this strange world of ours.

Good luck, and I will hear through my human sources what you decided to do.

This will be my last message to you until the war has either started or ended.

Good luck!

CHAPTER FIFTEEN

Atia took control of the meeting. "We are just coming off of a terrible defeat and all the people of the Neanderthal and human worlds will be thinking that all things should stay pretty quiet around here for a very long time as we try to recover from the terrible beating that we just took.

"Here are some of my thoughts, and we shall talk about them, and any ideas that you might want to share. Then we'll take a vote upon any actions that we might wish to take. We have to be completely united, and only if we act together can we defeat our enemies.

"I am suggesting that we send Mog another secret letter, only this time that letter will be our letter, and it will have Mog doing things the way that we want him to, and hopefully we can lead him into a trap. I want to use his plan of using insider information against him and turn things completely around for our benefit. I suggest that we do this quickly while the glow of victory is still upon the Neanderthals.

"Mog and his people will not be suspecting anything like this from us, since it was the last insider letter that he received from his own insider, our general, that turned the tide of battle his way and allowed him to gain his victory.

"I believe we lost to Mog not because he was smarter or more prepared than we were, but because he knew in advance what our weaknesses were.

"We have to learn from him and play this deadly game by his rules. We have to learn to lie and cheat, or, in other words, we have to learn to think like a Neanderthal!

"We have to strike while this fire is hot, or we will lose the edge that we might just have right now. Now here are my thoughts...."

IC IC-IE

While that very secret of meetings was going on in the mountain retreat for several days, a very unhappy Mog had just walked out of a wasted hour of his time talking to his General Army Staff.

He should have known that there would not be one original thought among them. Not one new or interesting idea was even brought up—and these were the best leaders that he could find.

It did not look good to him that when it came to having a new and original thought, he was the only one who could think out of the box of the old tried-and-true ways of doing things exactly as Neanderthals had been doing for generations beyond number.

He walked out of the meeting to clear his head and stormed off alone except for his faithful bodyguards, who went wherever he went.

Another sad thing that bothered him was that he had allowed all the human females to be used as shields, and there was not one of them around when he wanted them. All he could do was head back to his offices located on the front edge of the encampment, and it was there that he received a surprise that started him on a new plan of action that once again had him excited.

When. he entered his private living space he saw an arrow with a message attached to it from his own private spy, the general.

A big smile crossed his face as he worked carefully at removing the arrow that was deeply embedded into the wooden wall. He was hoping that the letter would tell him what was going on inside the enemy settlement, since the humans were last seen just running away from the battlefield.

It was with great pleasure that he carefully unwrapped the thick letter and placed it on the center of his desk.

He poured himself something strong to drink and settled down for what he hoped was an interesting hour of intense reading material. His mood had changed once again, and he was now a happy Neanderthal.

CHAPTER SIXTEEN

Hello, Mog:

Well, you really, really surprised me! I knew you were one smart Neanderthal but you really impressed the hell out of me. I did not think that you could think your way out of the trap that supreme leader Atia seemed to have you in. Well, you surely beat them all, didn't you?

You had them running away by the hundreds—this was hard to believe, and if I had not seen it with my own eyes, I would not have believed that it was possible.

Right now, Atia and all the other human leaders are so depressed that I think that they are ready to give up and accept your last offer of dividing the world up into parts—one being human and one being Neanderthal.

I was invited, with all of the other human leaders, to meet with Supreme Leader Atia at one of their hidden meeting places up high in the local mountains that is surrounded on two sides by deep canyons and can only be found by means of a very secret underground passageway that I never heard about.

I believe that this is your chance to end the war with one final battle. What if I was able to tell you the what, when and the where of the location, and who was going to be there? With this knowledge in advance of the meeting, you could set up all types of traps and wipe out all of the human leaders at one time.

I, of course, will excuse myself so that I can be gone elsewhere—spending the many valuable coins and things that you will be giving me for the information.

And now, this is most important! I have seen up close and personal how some of your generals were not capable of carrying out the easiest of orders, and screwed up the field battles at your end. You had better be present to direct things yourself because if things don't go well for your Neanderthals with this attack, the human leaders will never again all be together at one place, and I will be long gone, and they will know that it was me who sold them out.

This means you will never get the information I always gave to you, and you will never know what is really going on without me.

This has to be a perfect Neanderthal operation and unless you are leading the soldiers, something will screw up like it always does.

I will be sending you one last letter with all the details you will need, after you deposit my ill-gotten gains in the usual place.

If you listen to my ideas here, I can see a world with Neanderthals as masters of the known world, and humans, both male and female, as slaves to do your bidding forever and ever.

I leave you now with the reminder that you will never hear from me again after you pay me my reward and I give you the specific information you will need to become the master of the entire world that I know you want to be.

And my last comment here is that you need not worry that I will take your rewards that you will leave for me and disappear. I know that if I lie or cheat you, and do not deliver to you what I promise to deliver to you (the time-date-location and who will be there), my life will be taken from me, because you would search for me to the very end of time.

My fear for my life will make all of the information that I get you one hundred percent accurate.

Best of luck and start putting together my pay-off, because the gathering of the human leaders is coming up very soon.

I wish you a nice life!

CHAPTER SEVENTEEN

The Neanderthals' supreme leader, Mog, sat quietly at his reading desk.

He must have read and re-read the human general's latest letter, sent to him by the usual secret route, at least a dozen times, and he was still in a complete state of puzzlement.

Mog was fully aware that this letter was the seventh one that he had received within the last year. To be sure that it was his inside contact who sent him this letter, he checked it out against the other letters for the ink and the handwriting style. There was no doubt that this was sent to him by the general, and so he had opened it and read the puzzling message.

Mog was always pleased to receive his insider's secret messages because it kept him up to date as to what the humans were doing. The general's letters up to this moment were always absolutely accurate in every detail and in every bit of advice that he had given.

But something about the timing or perhaps the wording used by the general in this new letter did not seem to feel just right to Mog.

Then again, the general might have been in a great hurry or under some sort of time pressure to get this letter off to him. That would account for the little difference in his writing style, and Mog was prepared to overlook it.

Mog was rather surprised by what the general was telling him, and something inside Mog told him that this letter was not what it was supposed to be. His feelings about something that made him uncomfortable like this had saved his life many times, and he needed to think about what the general was telling him here.

Mog did not doubt that the general was absolutely well informed because, after all, he was on the second-highest level of leadership after the supreme leader Atia himself.

What was bothering Mog was that the general was sounding much too eager to get Mog himself involved in what he was proposing.

Never had the general ever suggested a plan of action that involved Mog personally as did this one! This created a warning flag in Mog's ever-suspicious mind.

Mog knew that he had a problem here. He liked the plan that the general was suggesting, but was not comfortable with his having to get personally involved.

It was true what the general said: each time that something important was given to one of Mog's men to carry out, something always got screwed up. Maybe the general was right, and it was time for him to get involved in finishing off the humans rather than sending another Neanderthal to do the job. There just was not a really bright Neanderthal who could step up and follow Mog's directions exactly as needed.

And so Mog had concluded that the general's plan to finish off the leadership of the humans was either a wonderful plan that he needed to jump on immediately, or it was a terrible disaster in the making. He decided that a decision could wait a few days. He knew that he needed to go over the pros and cons of what was being asked of him.

It was at moments like this that he missed his old female human advisor, Kat. They could have kicked around all the possibilities and come up with the right answer. But she was dead, and he had no one else to talk to. He would have to think the matter through himself. He would take the time to allow the idea of wiping out the entire leadership of the human race to run through his thought processes.

Always when some deep inner thinking was needed from him, Mog knew that the relaxation given to him by making love to a female was needed right now. Since there were no human females around after he had used them all up as protection for his men, he would have to look around for someone that was a purebred Neanderthal female.

The looking for someone to spend some quality time with was most of the fun!

CHAPTER EIGHTEEN

Mog could smell her fragrance. Subtle perfume, soap, clean skin and clean cotton.

Her hair fell to her collarbone as the shoulder seams on her undergarment stood up a little and made enticing shadowy tunnels. She was slim and well-toned, except where she shouldn't be, and she did not talk a lot! Mog liked a woman who gave him the minimum of chatter and went about her business with him.

Mog leaned forward and kissed her, just lightly on the lips. Her mouth was open a little and was cool and sweet from the wine.

He slid his free hand under her hair to the back of her neck. He then pulled her closer and kissed her a bit harder!

She did the same thing with her free hand

And they held the clinch for a whole minute, kissing while they balanced two wine glasses carefully in midair. Then they carefully parted and put their glasses down on the nearby table.

She leaned in and kissed him again, using both hands, one behind his head, and the other behind his back.

He did the same thing, symmetrically. Her tongue was cool and quick. Her back was narrow and her skin was warm. He slid his hand under her shirt and felt her hands beginning to drag out his shirt from his waistband. He liked the feel of her nails as they scratched gently against his skin.

"I don't usually do this," she said as her mouth was working hard against his, "not to people I work for."

"We're not working," he said. "We're taking a break."

She raised her arms over her head and held the pose as he pulled her covering off. She was wearing a tiny black bra and not much else.

Mog raised his huge arms in turn, and she knelt on the bed and pulled his shirt up and over his head. She threw his shirt into the same pile as her covering top.

She spread her hands on the very broad slab of his chest, and then she ran her hands down to his waist and undid his belt.

He unclipped her bra and carefully lifted her up and laid her down flat on the wide bed and gently kissed her full breasts.

Before either of them realized it they were in the bed, naked under the covering sheets and locked together, making love with a kind of patience and tenderness that neither of them had experienced for a long time.

"Neanderthal women," she said with a wide smile on her ugly face, "we have been around for a long, long time, and are well worth the wait."

Mog did not answer her. He just smiled and continued doing just what it was that he was doing.

CHAPTER NINETEEN

ANOTHER SIDEBAR NOTE
FROM AUTHOR BUD SELIGSON

efore we continue with our narrative on the rise and fall of the Neanderthal nation, an important written item has just been brought to my attention and it is of the utmost interest to all of us who are involved in the human/Neanderthal historical drama that has played itself out for so many years.

My very dear friend and honored copy editor Beth Shindler gave me a fascinating article recently written by a science writer for the *Los Angeles Times.* The date is February 20, 2016 and the writer is Deborah Netburn.

SCIENCE FILE

It's been 40,000 years since the Neanderthals disappeared, but their lingering genetic legacy may be influencing your health.

If-you are of Asian or European descent, about 2% of your genome came from Neanderthal ancestors, scientists say.

B2 SATURDAY, FEBRUARY 20, 2016   **Los Angeles Times**

MICHAEL SMELTZER Vanderbilt University

FOR MODERN humans of Asian and European heritage, about 2% of the genome comes from Neanderthal ancestors. A new study looks at how this affects health, including skin disease and fighting infection.

SCIENCE FILE

NEANDERTHALS' GENETIC LEGACY

Modern health issues have 40,000-year-old roots

Now, new evidence suggests this inheritance affects a broad range of health issues including skin disease, ability to fight infection and even risk of addiction and depression.

"Some of the associations we found made a lot of sense when we saw them, but the ones that affected neurological and psychiatric traits—these were surprising," said Tony Capra, a computational geneticist at Vanderbilt University in Nashville who oversaw the research.

About 50,000 years ago, the anatomically modern

humans who left Africa encountered many Neanderthal settlements somewhere in the Middle East, scientist believe.

The question of whether the two groups interbred was debated in scientific circles for decades until 2010, when researchers found clear evidence of Neanderthal DNA sequences in people alive today.

Since then, the genetic archaeologists have been trying to determine what instructions these Neanderthal genes contain code for, and why they have been preserved over so many millenniums.

The new study, published this month in the journal *Science,* is based on data collected by the e-merge network, which included the medical records and DNA sequences of 28,000 people in the United States.

The researchers also worked with a previously published map of all the places in the human genome where tenetic variants derived from Neanderthals have been found.

Armed with these two data sets, the team analyzed the genes of each of the 28,000 people in the consortium and determined whether they had any known signatures of Neanderthal DNA.

Then they looked for patterns that would indicate whether having these Neanderthal variants meant a person was more or less likely to have been diagnosed with a specific disease.

It stands to reason that the Neanderthal versions of genes would function differently from their modern human counterparts.

After all, Neanderthals had been living in northern latitudes for thousands of years before anatomically modern humans arrived, giving the Neanderthals plenty of time to adapt to the unique environment and pathogens.

Most geneticists believe that at least some of the Neanderthal DNA variants that remain in human genome were able to spread because they provided some advantage to our ancestors after they left Africa.

"We know when you move a population into a new environment, the bodily systems that are involved directly with that environment are most likely to change quickly," Capra said.

Indeed, the strongest signal the researchers found involved a Neanderthal variant that improves the blood's ability to coagulate or clot.

Today, too much clotting is considered a disorder because it increases risk of stroke, pulmonary embolisms and pregnancy complications.

But tens of thousands of years ago, this hypercoagulation might have served our ancestors well.

"Coagulation is one of the first immune responses the body has to a wound," Capra said.

A clot not only stops bleeding, it also sends messages to the immune system to join the fight against pathogens.

He added that the ability to form a scab quickly would have been useful for keeping unfamiliar germs out of the body.

The researchers also discovered an association between Neanderthal versions of genes and keratosis, a skin growth that can form after too much exposure to the sun.

Keratosis is caused by a dysfunction in a type of cell called a keratinocyte that protects the skin from ultraviolet sun rays and radiation.

However, in the low-light conditions of the north,

this mistake might have allowed more light to reach the skin, enhancing the production of vitamin D, Capra said.

Other findings were more difficult to explain.

For example, the study variants were associated with an increased risk of mood disorders and tobacco addiction, and also had a relatively strong effect on depression.

The idea that neurological and psychiatric traits are influenced by Neanderthal DNA is one of the most intriguing conclusion of the study, said Rasimus Nielsen, who studies evolutionary theory and genetics at UC–Berkeley.

This is interesting because it suggests that there were more differences in those traits between humans and Neanderthals than in other traits, suggesting perhaps that we are somewhat different from the Neanderthal traits that we inherited in the past.

The researchers also found that Neanderthal DNA variants had a subtle but real association with disorders including obesity, respiratory infections and coronary atherosclerosis or hardening of the arteries.

However, in these cases the Neanderthal variants account for less than 1% of the overall risk.

It was also noted that it is possible that we acquired many good traits from our Neanderthal relatives, although we presently do not know exactly which ones.

CHAPTER TWENTY

The meeting was once again called to order by Atia; and all the members of the organizing committee gave him their full attention as he stood quietly in the front center of the room.

"Once again I wish to thank you all for being here. I know that it is an inconvenience asking you to drop everything else that you all were doing in order to travel here again to our private meeting place, but I believe you will all agree with me that it will all be worth any sacrifice that we have to make if we can end the Neanderthal problem once and for all.

"This is our third and final meeting, and we have to leave here with a conclusive plan or our way of life will be at an end. Mog will see to it that we will never be able to rise up against the Neanderthal if we fail. It is now or never, and here is what we have going for us.

"We all remember quite clearly the letter we sent to Mog, to which we signed our turncoat general's name. We now know officially that the letter was received by Mog, because he left the gold and silver asked for in the general's letter as his reward for the special information he provided Mog.

"Mog left a letter of his own with the valuables for the general, and it is my understanding that this had never happened before. I am always worried when Mog does something new! I would like to think that this is a good thing, but with Mog, we never really know.

"Did he read the letter and believe all the things we told him? Did he become suspicious of some of the things we asked him to do, such as getting personally involved and have him going to several different locations?

"We are dealing with a most intelligent being, and we must not rely on Mog reacting to things the way most individuals would.

"I have had a copy made of the reply letter that Mog left for us with his payment to the general. If the general had received his payoff, he would have been a very rich man. I have turned over the valuable metals to our armed forces to help with some of their ongoing expenses. Mog would not be too happy if he knew that his valuables were going to be used against him.

"I would like to turn your attention now to the copy of Mog's letter that I made for each of you. I will read it out loud and comment on important issues as they are brought up by our great enemy, Supreme Leader Mog."

In a slow and deliberate voice, Atia began to read Mog's reply. The room was absolutely silent as he began.

Hello, General:

When you count up the gold and silver that I left for you, you will see that an extra bonus has been added to your ill-gotten gains. The extra valuables are there because I have always found your friendship and the vital information you have given to me to be most reliable and helpful. This gift to you from me is just my way of saying thank you for selling out your fellow humans.

Since this is the last letter that will pass between us, I just wanted you to know that I appreciate all that you have done for the Neanderthal cause!

Atia stopped reading the note, paused for a moment or two and then spoke again:

"I could not understand why the general would sell out his fellow humans to the Neanderthals, and I had a very private investigation carried out by my bodyguard, X, who is very good at this sort of thing.

"Without going into any of the unpleasant details that X's report uncovered, let me tell you that our general came to us from an outlying human settlement that was lost to us many years ago, due to what we thought was a Neanderthal war party.

"The general was only a young child of about ten years old who was hidden by his mother in a secret basement during the attack on the settlement where he lived with his parents and two older sisters.

"From his hiding place, the general was able to see the slaughter that wiped out every human within that entire settlement.

"It was the general who saw that the attackers were a large band of humans, who were welcomed freely into the settlement and spent a few days among the settlement people.

"It was a few nights later that these evil humans attacked, and killed every man, woman and child in the settlement, who believed that they were safe inside their stockade walls.

"It was our fellow humans who turned out to be worse than the beast-men that we call Neanderthals, as they butchered their own people, took all their valuables and weapons and went on their way.

"They were very clever in that they left evidence that pointed to the Neanderthals as the attackers.

"Our general, who never came out of hiding until the enemy humans had left, never told anyone what he saw.

"He must have carried this hatred for humans within himself for all those years as he worked his way up the human chain of command, from where he plotted against humanity.

"Of course, we do not agree with his choice of getting revenge against all humans for the terrible things done to his loved ones, but we might be able to offer him some understanding how these terrible events made him into the bitter man he is now.

"To this day, we never knew who those human killers were, and they could be anyone and anywhere around us.

"It only goes to prove that humans can be just as bad as the Neanderthals, and we had better put our thinking onto how to create a society where we can protect the innocent and punish the bad humans, just as we seek to punish the evil Neanderthals now.

"The general's story goes right to the heart of what we are fighting for. Justice and the right to live as a free people for all humans as long as they can be taught to live within the limits of human rights and human justice.

"And now let me put the case of our general aside,

and get on with the letter from Supreme Leader Mog."

Atia picked up his papers and continued to read:

I have to tell you, General, that I had some doubts and real issues with some of the things you suggested in your last letter to me. I was very curious about why you wanted me involved in two personal situations when you never had me involved before.

I decided to put your thoughts and suggestions to the test on the first situation and you came out one hundred percent perfect.

I am sorry I doubted you! You passed the Mog test, and the extra valuables I left you show my gratitude.

By now I am sure that you realize that the first of the two situations were the attack on myself that you warned me in advance about. This was the attack directed at me by your supreme leader Atia's nephew James. By knowing that he was personally coming after me, I was able to plan an escape route and obviously, since I am writing you this final letter, I escaped the plot on my life from this James fellow.

Now that I know your words are true, I will take personal action on the second part of your plan to kill the entire council of human leaders along with Supreme Leader Atia! With them all gone at the same time, I will be able to sweep over the puny humans, who will be leaderless and helpless before my army of Neanderthals.

And now I bid you a safe journey to wherever it is that you plan to go.

CHAPTER TWENTY-ONE

Atia looked around the entire room once more before he gathered himself and began to speak. "I can tell by the absolute silence now holding forth in this meeting room that you all understand quite clearly that we have accomplished the first difficult step of our plan to terminate Supreme Leader Mog.

"The general's letter that we wrote to Mog laid out several options for Mog to accept or reject. We all knew that he would have second thoughts, but we guessed correctly that he would try out the plans of part one and two before he did the last and most important part three, where his own life and safety would be actually threatened.

"The first test that Mog reluctantly agreed to was to allow my nephew James and his small band of soldiers to fight their way to one of his special hiding places, where he would know that James was coming after him in order to make an attempt at killing him. Mog and James did meet face to face for a few minutes before Mog made good on his personal escape plan that he had ready.

"Mog believed that we humans would not allow

so many good soldiers to die if the information given to him by the general was not accurate. James lost well over four hundred of our best human fighters in order to make Mog believe in the information that we sent to him with the general's name signed to make it seem real.

"So, part one of the plan was to try to kill Mog if James and his band were able to get to him through enemy lines. If only we could have had this evil Neanderthal killed, we would have achieved our endgame right there and then. But, as we all know, things did not work out in our favor, and James had to finally return and report the defeat to me, which he did.

"As planned, we allowed the news of the attempt on Mog's life to get out. Everyone knew that my nephew James was a great warrior, and a great man in his own right, and that he was so upset with the failure of his plan to succeed that he sent a personal message of his own to Mog, care of the Neanderthal settlement where we knew Mog spent his down-time.

"In this letter, delivered by several of our own soldiers under a white flag of truce, were angry words written by James in his own handwriting, challenging Mog to a one-on-one sword duel to determine who was the better man.

"It was my nephew James who came up with this three-part plan for the ultimate elimination of Mog as the hoped-for final outcome. James put his own life on the line and sadly it was James who ended up dying, but by so doing, he set up Mog for his elimination in the final steps of our master plan. Let me review the three steps for you as suggested to us and accepted by myself from James.

"Step one was to be James's attack with his five-hundred-strong attacking force of warriors, on a minor stronghold where we knew Mog would be on a specific date. We all know how badly that turned out, with our losing over four hundred of our best warriors—and Mog escaped from the clash of arms, as he always does.

"Step two was for James to challenge the manhood of supreme leader Mog, with a very personal offer to meet him in a duel to the death between the two of them. Of course, the note was sent, and Mog accepted the personal challenge, and sadly my nephew not only lost this one-on-one fight, but also his life. James' defeat and his ultimate death are very important factors to help us get Mog to the right moment at the right place where we want him to be, which we believe will be the death of him.

"And now let me read to you the sad but true description of the battle between Supreme Leader Mog and my nephew James. The notes that I will be reading to you now were written by the man that we hid in an overlooking cave as he watched the fight between James the human and Mog the Neanderthal."

My name is Dava, and I am one of the personal scribes assigned to supreme leader Atia. Atia asked for a volunteer for this dangerous assignment, and I was chosen from among the six of us who stepped up.

I am writing this note as I lie here quietly waiting for events to happen just below my vantage point. I am covered over with leaves and branches just in case someone is looking for someone like me.

I can see in the distance two male figures

approaching the flat fighting area where they had agreed to meet. Each of them is alone, and as they get closer I can see that they each are carrying a long spear, a sword that is strapped down to their side, and several long knives that appear to be secured by tied-down holding sheaths.

I can see each of them clearly now as they step up to the edge of the large, flattened dirt area which was where they would do battle.

I must note here something that I find very strange. Here is Mog, supreme leader of the entire Neanderthal nation, sitting down quietly in the middle of the fighting area. He is looking at James, the hero of the human forces, right in the eye as they each take out a smoking pipe of some sort and light them up. The appearance is one of two friends sitting together and enjoying each other's company, instead of two fighting men who will shortly be trying to kill each other.

I must say that this is a most civilized thing that I am seeing right there before my eyes. Here is this huge and extremely dangerous-looking Neanderthal sitting and talking with another dangerous-looking but much smaller human, and it almost looks like they are enjoying whatever it was that the two of them were talking about. If I did not know that they were shortly going to try and kill each other, I would say that they were two friends talking about the day's hunt or some other interesting tidbit.

I am utterly in shock over these things going on below me that are so peaceful and civilized. I will be holding my breath until this free-for-all and no-holds-barred fight begins. I am beside myself with anxiety and desire to see how this unbelievable event will happen.

CHAPTER TWENTY-TWO

The time had finally arrived and both men realized it and slowly rose to their feet and stood about five feet away from each other upon the flattened earthen fighting area that they had agreed upon as being their battle-field. From my vantage point of looking down upon the two combatants, I became acutely aware of the tremendous difference in the size of the two of them.

The Neanderthal stood at about five foot five inches, while his taller and much slimmer opponent looked to me as being about five foot nine or ten, and possibly weighing in at one hundred eighty pounds to Supreme Leader Mog's estimated weight of possibly close to two hundred and fifty pounds.

To my extremely prejudiced eye, James looked like the picture of a god that I always carried in my mind. He was tall for a human; slender, blond-haired, with muscles that rippled when he moved. He seemed, to me, to be the perfect specimen of a human male, as opposed to the beast-man who slowly began circling around him. Supreme Leader Mog was extremely grotesque and ugly. I know that I am prejudiced in my physical description of the two of them, but I am only human, and I am reporting things as I see them through my own eyes and through my own perspective.

From my perch high above the two of them, it was extremely difficult to judge this sort of thing, but it was not hard to marvel at the great skill that each of the two men brought to their match. My eyes followed their movements as they slowly began to circle each other in the standard clockwise circular motion so that the swords that they held in their right hands were always held out in front of them. They seemed ready to engage at any moment as they carefully judged the other's circling moves.

Suddenly, with no warning, Mog's sword leaped out at James, who quickly jumped back as the razor-sharp sword drew a fine red line across his naked chest. James danced backwards, his broadsword flickering at Mog to keep him away as he recovered from the surprise of how quickly Mog and his blade were able to move. Mog continued his slow advance, catching each sword thrust made by James upon the safety handle of his sword.

It seemed to my eye, looking down on the two of them, that this match would soon be over. James appeared to be overmatched with the quicker-moving, stronger Mog, who was completely on the offensive. Mog made five or six strong and straight thrusts against the retreating James that caused him to keep giving up ground as he tried to defend himself against his bigger, stronger and faster opponent.

James' right shoulder dipped slightly as he was getting ready to try an offensive thrust against Mog, but he was too slow. With a blinding thrust Mog ran his sword through the right sword arm of James, who dropped his sword as Mog's weapon entered deeply into his shoulder.

James retreated a few feet, fell backward and just lay there helplessly looking up at the Neanderthal, who stood there with a snarl on his face. Seeing that the blood was seeping from the deep and open wound, Mog turned his back on James, gathered up his belongings and disappeared into the forest from where I first saw him appear. I was still up in my perch looking down as I saw Mog disappear into the surrounding brush.

I went as fast as I could to try and get down from the cave so that I could help James, but within the many minutes that it took for me to get to the battleground, James had already pulled himself up and disappeared from sight.

It took me many long minutes until I was able to pick up his trail. I am not among the world's best trackers, and it took me perhaps fifteen minutes until I caught up with James, whom I found lying there dead in a large pool of his own blood.

He was looking skyward, and in his left hand was a parchment that had writing on it. I could see that it was written in blood, and this message from James, who had written the following words in his own blood, made no sense to me at all.

I put the message into my carryall and promptly buried James right where he was lying.

Then, as instructed, I turned and followed the path that would lead me back to where Supreme Leader Atia would be waiting for me.

I was extremely sad that I was the one who had to tell Atia about the outcome of the fight and deliver the message that James had sent to him written in his own blood.

CHAPTER TWENTY-THREE

Atia looked around the entire room once again, waited for the upcoming silence and began to speak in his soft voice that continued to carry well across the entire room.

"My family and I will privately mourn the loss of my nephew James, who died bravely to get us vital information on Mog the Killer. Our well-hidden observer brought me back a parchment written out by James with only two code words written on it.

It is a wonder that he was able to survive the attack of the beast-man long enough to write this message, but he did, and I will read you the message he left for me that will allow us to complete the plan that will allow us to destroy Supreme Leader Mog.

By the way, I call this plan very simply MOG MUST DIE!

Remember, part one of the three-part plan was to have Mog believe in the general's fake letter we sent with three steps in it.

We have already competed step one, where James and his five hundred mounted soldiers tried to kill him in his mountain retreat and failed. James returned with only about fifty of the original five hundred soldiers, and their deaths and Mog's easy escape from his attempted killing made a believer of Mog.

The one-on-one duel that ended up with the loss of my nephew to Mog was part two of the plan. Mog accepted our theory that we would never plan to lose over four hundred of our mounted soldiers to him, and never would he believe that James gave up his life to get Mog to accept the second step of the plan.

Yes, we lost the soldiers and yes, we lost James, but according to the note that James was able to get back to me, we now have the proof we needed to put the third and final part of the plan into action. James' words on the last message he would ever send out were "Mog believes!"

Based upon those two words written by James, I hereby order us to move forward into the final stage of our plan. We now will move into the third and final stage, and here is how we will do it.

CHAPTER TWENTY-FOUR

Supreme Leader Mog was the happiest Neanderthal in all of his known world. He had escaped an attempt on his life when five hundred mounted horse soldiers had barged into his secret hideaway. He, of course, had expected the attack, since he had the letter from his friend the General to guide him, and everything had gone according to plan.

The attempt failed, and they wiped out over four hundred of the best human horse-soldiers, and he was able to do it by buying the services of the human general once again.

His source of secret information got better and better when the general told him that as part of the human plan was the part that their best warrior, called James something or other, was going to challenge him to a private duel.

He had accepted the duel and easily had killed off that James fellow. He was feeling really good about that, but best of all was when the general laid out the final part of his letter by telling him where and when Supreme Leader Atia and his military staff were going up to a secret mountain hideaway to plan a big push against the Neanderthals. The general had given him plenty of advance notice as to where, when and how to encircle and trap the human leaders and end this human-Neanderthal war once and for all. The general's information was the final missing piece of information that he lacked to wipe out his enemy once and for all, and he was happy beyond belief.

He had given his orders to his generals, and it would take a few months to get everything ready for the month of July, when the human meeting was to take place. He had plenty of time to go over and over every tiny detail of his planned Neanderthal attack on the human hideout, and he was pleased that he now had everything set in motion for the big. day.

And as usual when he was happy and excited and his planning did not need his immediate attention, his thoughts turned to his sex life, and he was ready to get out there and get some female companionship.

His problem, and it was a nice problem, was that there were hardly any human female captives left in the entire settlement. He had pretty much used them up in his brilliant move of using them as shields when he had sent the humans back where they came from in a complete and glorious victory for himself and his Neanderthal armed forces.

He dressed up and thought he looked great and went out.

CHAPTER TWENTY-FIVE

She kissed him back as she wrapped herself around him with her arms and legs. As best she could, anyway in her current position, as he held her tightly as well, pulling her against him and levering her at an angle for the deepest access, the longest strokes and the most pleasure.

His hips pistoned between her legs as he thrust into her, pumping so hard that the rough fabric of the cheap room's bed cover chafed her bare skin as he drove her inch by inch across the huge and well-used bed. But the slight discomfort only seemed to heighten her pleasure and drew every glimmer of her attention to the most indescribable sensations completely rocking through her system.

She was already so close to meltdown that his very next touch sent her off like a rocket. Her skin prickled and tiny dots of color burst behind her closed eyelids as wave after wave of pure unadulterated ecstasy rolled through her. Her back was aching, and her nails were digging into his broad shoulders, as she opened up her mouth to scream only to have Mog cover her mouth with his once again.

He continued to drive into her, his thrusts growing shorter and harder. "Yes," he huffed, his cheeks brushing hers, his face turning into the curve of her smooth neck. "Yes, yes, yes!" he screamed. And then he completed his act, erupting inside her with a hoarse bellow that seemed to shake the entire room.

The sound echoed in her ears and through the small, dingy room. As thin as the walls of that place probably were, she wouldn't have been very surprised if all of the other guests in the establishment had heard him, too. Not that she cared! At that moment in time, she was too relaxed and felt too content to care about much of anything.

Mog's weight continued to press her into the worn mattress, making it difficult for her to catch her breath. But instead of shifting her body around, or asking him to move, she wanted to stay this way as long as possible. She wanted to luxuriate in his hard and blatant masculinity, in the sensation of him still filling her, still making her feel like an attractive, desirable woman. He was Mog! And she knew him for who and what he was, and he could do to her whatever it was that he wanted.

All too soon, however, he started to roll away, but before she could heave a sigh of regret, he encircled her waist once again and pulled her toward him. He arranged them so that his head rested on one of the pillows near the headboard, and she was draped on top of him like a warm, boneless and completely sated blanket.

Just as she was beginning to drift off on a cloud of satisfaction that she hadn't experienced in a very, very long time, his chest rumbled beneath her cheek, and his chin dug into the crown of her head. "Don't get comfortable," he murmured. "I'm not finished with you yet!"

CHAPTER TWENTY-SIX

The large cabin was absolutely silent, and all that could be heard was the slow and deep breathing of the four men who were sharing their time and their interest in the project that they all had on their minds, called *Mog Must Die.*

Present were Atia, the acknowledged Supreme Leader of the united forces of humanity, his twenty-two-year-old son, Anoti, who was seen by one and all as next in line for his father's job, X, who had come out of his early retirement to take over security for the project, and a new up-and-coming young man who had the all-important job of coordinating the cavalry, foot soldiers, archers, spearmen, and all the other fighting men and women who were now rounding out the numbers of the human forces.

X was entertaining them with one of his radical points of view on the good and bad things of the life going on around them. X was saying: "a pessimist habitually sees and anticipates the worst, believes that we all live in a world of gloom and doom, and that there is more pain and evil in the world than goodness and happiness.

Conflict, death and destruction are three things that we all must deal with on a daily basis. From the very beginning, we humans have existed in utter chaos, and I marvel at how our lives were able to form, grow and evolve throughout all of this craziness.

"*Homo sapiens,* which is what we call ourselves, means 'wise, rational man.' What it should really mean is, how can I kill off the other guy and still remain pure and innocent? Ever since our ancestors, the cave men bashed a friend over the head with a rock, we rational being have been killing and slaughtering each other either individually or in droves. As our numbers grew, we banded together in ever-increasing groups which developed into settlements, and after this finally happened, it did not take *Homo sapiens* long to figure out that power is the name of the game— he who has the power can name the game.

"That bit of insight led to greater and greater confrontations, and to this very day, war is the way we solve our grievances. War is a method accepted by our civilized people, as long as we play this game of war by the rules.

"I fear for the human race after we rid the world of the Neanderthals! Then we will have only ourselves to war upon, and war upon each other we shall, as sure as we are all sitting here together.

"We will continue to forge new weapons, to make them more sophisticated, so that we will be able to kill more of our own kind with better and better weapons. We will probably advance past slingshots, spears and arrows, and even swords. Who knows what will be next? I shudder to even think of the years ahead of mankind once we clean things up here.

"We humans do not seem to be able to control the rage that lives within us, and we cannot seem to satisfy that part of our nature that desires power for ourselves and the submission of others. Could it possibly be that war is just an innate craving for human excitement? I believe that our mental powers are not strong enough to control our own emotions. Rational man is a paradox of many things.

"And speaking of a man of many things, I give you Mika, our newest and perhaps the greatest general of our armed forces. Welcome, Mika. I give you the floor and we are all very attentive to your upcoming report that will hopefully lead us down the path to the destruction of our great enemy, Mog."

ㅏℂ ℥⊹⟨Ɛ

Mika, a well-dressed young man of perhaps thirty years of age, nods politely at X and steps up to front of the room where all eyes are now looking at him. A big smile crosses his handsome face as he looks at each of the leaders of humanity who are present.

"Supreme Leader Atia, Anoti, and X! I look at the three of you and all my doubts disappear. I look at you and realize it is not just a mere hope that we have here, but a reality that we will make happen very shortly. That reality is, of course, the death of Supreme Leader Mog. This is the most important issue that has ever been brought up and discussed. With Mog alive and well, we are all aware that no matter what plans we make, or what weapons we keep coming up with, this one Neanderthal always comes up with a way to stop us and keep us on the defensive.

"The four of us have discussed the fact that, the way things are going, the Neanderthals will become the dominant race on our ever-shrinking planet. We humans, at best, will become second position to the beast-men, and it will only be a matter of time until they completely destroy us all. This is a foregone conclusion.

"I have been in deep discussion these last few days with Supreme Leader Atia, and I must state, for the record and for all of you to hear, that I agree one hundred percent with his plan to rid us of Mog, but I am not pleased with all of the four factors that he is putting into place, and who he has chosen to enforce them.

"The *who* of the plan, of course, is Mog, and we all agree that he must die, and that has to be sooner rather than later.

"The *what* of the plan is by using something called quicksand. Quicksand is something that I never heard of. I asked each of you if you knew what it was, and it was a negative from each of you. Only Leader Atia smiled and nodded when I told him what the quicksand report said. Leader Atia will go into the details in a few minutes on this quicksand thing.

"We now know that the who of our plan is to be Mog, and we know that the what of it is to be quicksand, whatever that is. The next of the 'four W questions' (that is, who, what, when and where) is *when* and leader Atia tells me that the when is to be within the new two weeks.

"The fourth W is *where*, and that is what Atia will talk about as soon as I stop talking. I am going to read you the short research paper that I gave to Leader Atia, so that it will be clear in our minds what exactly Atia is going to be talking about, and how it relates to the destruction of Mog. Here is the information on what our best researchers have come up with on supreme leader Atia's request. I will read the report in full so you can be as confused as I am."

My name is Rons, and I have been working as a record keeper for Supreme Leader Atia. I have been asked by him to investigate the special kind of ground that is referred to as quicksand. I have been working on this project for Leader Atia for a long time now and can confidently say that I know all that there is to know about this subject. Here are three ways of talking about this very different physical property.

The room was absolutely still as Mika shuffled his papers around as he found his spot and he again began to read in his clear sounding voice.

Quicksand is a saturated sediment that looks solid until a weight causes it to lose strength, and anything falling into it will quickly sink below the surface. Quicksand forms when loose dirt and sand are suddenly agitated when water in the sand can't escape, so it creates a liquefied soil that loses strength and can't hold any weight. It is a loose, wet, deep sand deposit in which a person or heavy object may be easily engulfed.

After reading his report, Mika politely smiles at each of the leaders in the room and then quietly takes his leave.

CHAPTER TWENTY-SEVEN

Anoti, son of Atia, X, the strong and usually silent one, and Mika, the newly appointed head of all the armed forces, watched as Rons quietly closed the door behind him.

Atia was waiting for someone to say something, but since no one did, he took the lead as he always did. "Quicksand will do the job for us that clubs, spears and knives never could do when it came to Mog. The only problem is that we have to go to it rather than have the quicksand come to us. Let us put quicksand away for now.

"Let me finish telling you about the plan that my nephew James came up with, and that I approved. I have tried to keep all personal emotions out of everything connected to Mog but it is difficult. My hatred of the beast-man is so strong that it dominates my every living moment. Here is the end game that will ease my personal pain—and Mog's life.

"The general's letter set Mog up in two ways. It had correctly told Mog about the attempt on his life by the five hundred horsemen.

"Mog took the information and acted upon it. As a result, he escaped, but many of our top horsemen didn't. Mog must have been very happy with part one of the General's letter.

"Part two told him my nephew James would be challenging him to a personal duel. James issued the challenge and Mog defeated him in what we all understand was a fair fight.

"Since Mog reacted and responded to parts one and two of the letter we sent him, our best thinkers believe he will not hesitate to do whatever he has to do to be a success at part three.

"Hold your comments for a moment as I tell you part three, which I have ready to go. Please remember that we have all sworn to destroy Mog or die in the attempt. Here is how the truth of this pledge will play out.

"Part three of the letter that Mog now accepts as being from our traitor general tells him where I will personally be on a specific date that is rapidly approaching. Mog has put himself in harm's way each time we have moved him around, and we feel he will do so again so as to avoid any screw-up in his being able to get at me, his sworn worst enemy.

"I want you all to recall our last resort hideaway that we call Lake Forest. The only way to reach it is to traverse several very narrow paths that will only allow passage of one person at a time. Mog is aware that I will be alone at this location waiting for the leader of our fellow humans from the southern part of our territory.

"The pretext for the two of us meeting in this remote and out-of-the-way location is to avoid the possibility of anyone listening to the agreement that we are supposedly to work out, where they will pledge their fighting men to us in exchange for positions of leadership in the United Council of Humanity that we are planning to form.

"We believe that Mog will act on my being alone in an isolated place and come to attack me himself. He won't trust anyone else! The truth of the matter is that I *will* be alone.

"I will be alone and waiting for Mog because this is a suicide mission, and it is one that neither Mog nor I will walk away from.

"And before you all start screaming at me, let me say that without Supreme Leader Mog, the Neanderthals will vanish from the Earth, and without me, the humans will still grow and expand beyond all our dreams. I willingly give up my life to achieve this lofty goal, and what pleases me is that this plan is foolproof and is guaranteed to work. I am obviously quite willing to bet my life on it.

"And last, before you all start in on me, I wish to point out several things.

"Anoti, my son, had been trained well and will be able, with all of your help, to continue to guide our people to a new world without a Mog in it.

"X and you Mika, will join Anoti to form the council of three that I have already started setting up. It will be the job of this council to move humanity into the war of extermination of the Neanderthal.

"I now will shut my mouth and listen to you all scream at me. But I must warn you that I have already made peace with my wife Ana on all of this, and there is no way of turning me aside from doing these well-planned actions that are moving forward."

CHAPTER TWENTY-EIGHT

The days and weeks had flown by fast as Atia tried to clear up as much of the paperwork that went along with the job of Supreme Leader. He was going on the assumption that his next face-to-face meeting with Mog at the predetermined location in the highlands of the Alps would be his last.

He had gone back and forth to that special place in the mountains where the final meeting with Mog was being planned and had become familiar with every crack and divide that was on the path leading to and from the flat area at the top.

He had constructed a small cottage made quite simply to look like a meeting place. He did not want Mog to stay away from the top of the little mountain peak because something did not look right to him.

Atia was very careful not to let any information leak out about the location because if there was a secret meeting going to be held there, then a complete blackout would be in effect.

He wanted everything to appear normal when Mog made his move on the top side of the location.

Only the council of three and his wife Ana knew that the one path leading up to the top was packed with explosives that would completely destroy the path that led up and down the mountain.

If things went well, and Mog did come up to attack him, Atia was very sure that knowing that Atia was alone, Mog was sure to come at him! Mog would probably act very civilized, just as he had with James before he murdered him. The two of them, Mog and himself, would probably sit down and talk for a while before Mog would decide enough with the talking and on with the killing.

Atia believed that he would recognize when that moment would arrive, and at that time, he would light the tip of the fuse that would be buried in the ground next to where he would be sitting when Mog made his "surprise" entrance. What Mog would not know was that Atia was prepared to die. As long as Mog died with him, he would be a happy human being. Atia would light the quick-burning fuse that would blow up the only path going up or down from the mountain top where they would be sitting and talking.

With the path blown up, Mog would probably fly into a rage, and even though Atia would try to fight with Mog, who would most likely attack him within moments of the explosion, he knew that he would not be able to defeat Mog, and he realized that those moments were to be his last moments on earth.

With Atia dead and no way to follow a path down the mountain, Mog, who would have scouted out the area before going up to the top, would think that all he had to do was jump into the little lake that surrounded the high peak he was on. This would be the second part of Atia's death plan for Mog.

The first was that Mog would not know that the mountain path was lined with the newly discovered explosives, and secondly, when he would decide to escape from the mountain top by jumping into the little lake that looked so easy to splash-land into, and then swim to the nearby shore, his walking away a happy Neanderthal would never happen again! Not only would Mog not know about the explosives set to go off, but he would be unfamiliar with the water covering over that deadly material called quicksand.

Atia smiled to himself as he saw in his mind's eye Mog slowly and surely trying to get out of the slowly sinking quicksand, only to finally go under the surface and die a horrid and difficult death due to lack of oxygen. Atia could not think of a better way of killing off Mog than to make him suffer as he slowly died, inch by inch, trying to catch a breath of air as he sank into the depths of the death trap that had been waiting for him.

And finally, Atia smiled to himself, thinking that the new invention of explosives, that produced a volume of rapidly expanding gas destroying everything around it, would be the salvation of mankind, once they were rid of Supreme Leader Mog once and for all.

⟨ ⟩⟨ ⟨⟩

And just as it was foreseen by Atia, that is exactly the way the death of Mog the terrible—of Mog the beast-man—and Mog the most hated and brilliant of all the Neanderthals, died for lack of a little oxygen.

THANK YOU FOR THE READ!
SINCERELY—BUD SELIGSON

ABOUT THE AUTHOR

WHO IS THE REAL BUD SELIGSON?

Bud Seligson, who was born in Chicago, Illinois, has been a ghostwriter to many of the major well-known writers of today's fiction and science fiction. He is also well known in Hollywood as a "story doctor" for many studios. Bud lives in Los Angeles with his wife, Diane, who is his co-writer and sometime editor.